SHORT STORIES
OF
AURORA
RHAPSODY

THE COMPLETE COLLECTION

G. S. JENNSEN

HYPERNOVA
PUBLISHING
2017

Hypernova Publishing
174 E Neider Ave #89
Coeur d'Alene, ID 83815
www.hypernovapublishing.com

Publisher's Note: This is a work of fiction. Names, characters, places, and incidents are a product of the author's imagination. Locales and public names are sometimes used for atmospheric purposes. Any resemblance to actual people, living or dead, or to businesses, companies, events, institutions, or locales is completely coincidental.

The Hypernova Publishing name, colophon and logo are trademarks of Hypernova Publishing.

Ordering Information:
Hypernova Publishing books may be purchased for educational, business or sales promotional use. For details, contact the "Special Markets Department" at the address above.

Short Stories of Aurora Rhapsody: The Complete Collection /
G. S. Jennsen.—1st ed.

LCCN 2017961032
ISBN 978-0-9984245-8-3

CONTENTS

AMARANTHE UNIVERSE

AURORA RHAPSODY

AURORA RISING
STARSHINE
VERTIGO
TRANSCENDENCE

AURORA RENEGADES
SIDESPACE
DISSONANCE
ABYSM

AURORA RESONANT
RELATIVITY
RUBICON
REQUIEM

ASTERION NOIR

EXIN EX MACHINA
OF A DARKER VOID
THE STARS LIKE GODS

RIVEN WORLDS

CONTINUUM
INVERSION
ECHO RIFT

ALL OUR TOMORROWS
CHAOTICA
DUALITY

COSMIC SHORES

MEDUSA FALLING
THE THIEF
THE UNIVERSE WITHIN

SHORT STORIES

Restless, Vol. I • Restless, Vol. II • Apogee • Solatium • Venatoris
Re/Genesis • Meridian • Fractals • Chrysalis • Starlight Express

Learn more at gsjennsen.com/books or visit the
Amaranthe Wiki: gsj.space/wiki

AURORA RHAPSODY
TIMELINE

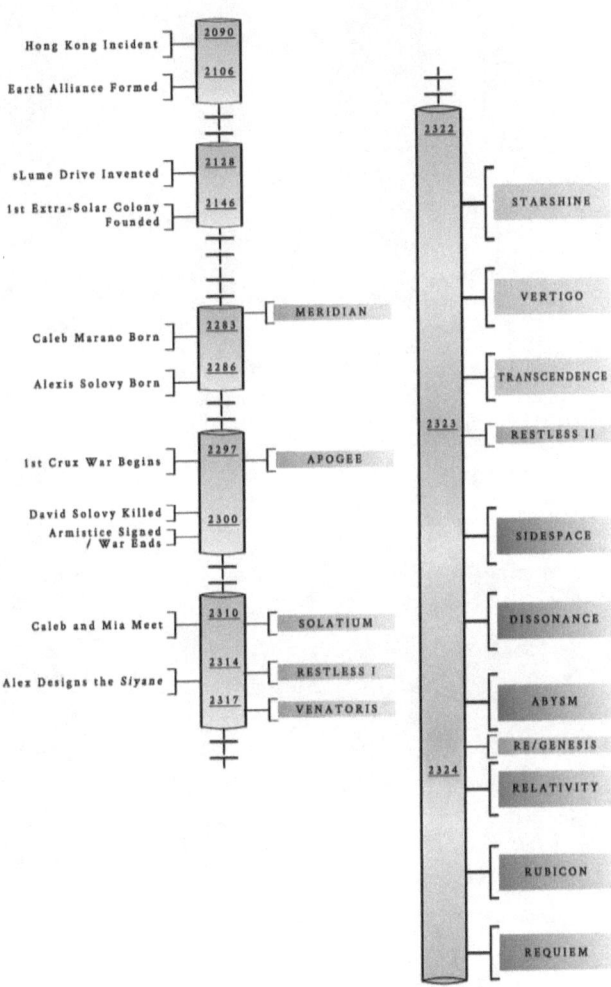

Hong Kong Incident — 2090

Earth Alliance Formed — 2106

sLume Drive Invented — 2128

1st Extra-Solar Colony Founded — 2146

Caleb Marano Born — 2283 — MERIDIAN

Alexis Solovy Born — 2286

1st Crux War Begins — 2297 — APOGEE

David Solovy Killed — 2300
Armistice Signed / War Ends —

Caleb and Mia Meet — 2310 — SOLATIUM

Alex Designs the *Siyane* — 2314 — RESTLESS I

2317 — VENATORIS

2322

2323

2324

STARSHINE

VERTIGO

TRANSCENDENCE

RESTLESS II

SIDESPACE

DISSONANCE

ABYSM

RE/GENESIS

RELATIVITY

RUBICON

REQUIEM

View the Timeline online at gsjennsen.com/aurora-rhapsody

COLONIZED WORLDS

●●●●●● **SENECAN FEDERATION TERRITORY**
○ **INDEPENDENT WORLDS**

WORLDS VISITED IN THE SHORT STORIES COLLECTION :

EARTH ALLIANCE
EARTH
ERISEN
RADAVI
SHI SHEN
- YUZHOU LI

SENECAN FEDERATION
SENECA
CAELUM
- PARNES

METIS NEBULA
PORTAL PRIME
AMARANTHE

INDEPENDENTS
ATLANTIS
PANDORA
ROMANE

MILKY WAY GALAXY

View the Colonized Worlds Map online at gsjennsen.com/map-shorts

A NOTE FROM THE AUTHOR

The world of *Aurora Rhapsody* spans five decades, megaparsecs of space and hundreds of exoplanets. Yet even with over a million words written across nine novels, there were more stories that needed to be told.

These are those stories.

Some, like *Apogee*, reveal events that have a significant impact on the plot and characters of *Aurora Rhapsody*. Others, like *Solatium*, reveal valuable insights into the history and motivations of those characters. None are required reading to enjoy the novels, but all add depth, nuance and greater understanding to them.

What order should these stories be read in? Well, that depends to some extent on where you are in reading the novels, but it's ultimately up to you.

The stories are presented here in publication order. If you like, you can simply read straight through—I've included a note at the beginning of each story which places it in context.

Or, you can read them in chronological order according to the timeline of the *Aurora Rhapsody* universe:

MERIDIAN - APOGEE - SOLATIUM - RESTLESS I
- VENATORIS - *Aurora Rising* - RESTLESS II -
Aurora Renegades - RE/GENESIS - *Aurora Resonant*

Or, if you're currently reading the novels and intend to read these alongside them, you can opt for my suggested reading order:

RESTLESS I - *Starshine* - SOLATIUM - *Vertigo* -
VENATORIS - *Transcendence* - RESTLESS II -
Sidespace - APOGEE - *Dissonance* - *Abysm* - RE/GENE-
SIS - *Relativity* - *Rubicon* - MERIDIAN - *Requiem*

This order is my subjective take on where each short story has the biggest impact on the overall plot of the novels, but it's only a suggestion. It is my hope that no matter the order you read them in, you will find them both entertaining and enlightening.

RESTLESS I

RESTLESS
VOL. I

AN
AURORA
RISING
SHORT STORY

G. S. JENNSEN

Space is vast and untamed, and it holds many secrets.
Now two individuals from opposite ends of settled space are on a collision course with the darkest of those secrets, even as the world threatens to explode around them.

…or they will be, in about 8 years. *Restless* is a short story prequel to *Starshine*, Book One of the *Aurora Rising* trilogy.

Before Alex Solovy was a successful interstellar scout, she was building starships and planning for the day when she would fly one she called her own. Before Caleb Marano was wiping out the terrorist group who murdered his mentor, he was…wiping out terrorist groups who murdered shopkeepers and threatened his friends.

Catch a glimpse of *Aurora Rising's* heroes while they were still becoming the individuals they will need to be in order to face the galactic threat which, for now, waits silently in the void.

*

Restless I was the first short story I wrote. It's full of major characters from the novels, including our heroes, Alex Solovy and Caleb Marano, as well as Kennedy Rossi and Mia Requelme. Restless I takes place a few years after Solatium but still eight years before Starshine. It tells the story of how Alex acquired her ship, the Siyane, while providing insight into a younger, decidedly rougher Caleb.

Since Restless I is intended to be an introduction into the world and characters of Aurora Rhapsody, it can be read at any time.

DRAMATIS PERSONAE

Alexis 'Alex' Solovy
Starship pilot, scout and space explorer;
daughter of Miriam and David Solovy.
Faction: *Earth Alliance*

Caleb Marano
Special Operations intelligence agent,
Senecan Federation Division of Intelligence.
Faction: *Senecan Federation*

Kennedy Rossi
Ship Designer, IS Design;
friend of Alex Solovy.
Faction: *Earth Alliance*

Mia Requelme
Businesswoman;
friend of Caleb Marano.
Faction: *Independent*

Samuel Padova
Special Ops, SF Intelligence;
mentor of Caleb Marano.
Faction: *Senecan Federation*

Miriam Solovy (Admiral)
EA North American Logistics Director;
mother of Alex Solovy, widow of David Solovy.
Faction: *Earth Alliance*

EARTH

SAN FRANCISCO

I quit.

Alex Solovy rolled the words around in her mind, trying out different inflections and intonations and generally letting her brain grow comfortable with the notion. Not so much the words themselves as what they signified.

Freedom, in all its wondrous and terrifying splendor.

She was on pleasant terms with her boss at Pacifica Aerodynamics—if not necessarily her coworkers—and bore him and the enterprise he operated no particular ill will. The opposite in fact; it was a decent company as companies went, inasmuch as it hadn't allowed two centuries worth of ship fabrication to weigh it down or stifle an innovative spirit.

No, unlike so many legions of corporate drones she wasn't quitting because she hated her job. She was quitting because the job had always been nothing more than a means to an end—a way to gain a fulsome understanding of and skill in operating every conceivable system to be found on a starship, plus each one's variations, quirks and maintenance requirements.

Two years before, she had left IS Design on Erisen because she had learned everything they had to teach her. Now she would leave Pacifica Aerodynamics for the same reason.

Seeing as they were the two premiere civilian starship manufacturers in the Earth Alliance, the only place where she could learn the remaining—and the most important—lessons was space itself.

She had also spent the previous four years of gainful employment saving every spare credit to pass through her account. Never one to spend frivolously on consumer trappings, she had trimmed her expenses to the bone by sharing a flat with Kennedy while on Erisen and, upon returning to San Francisco, renting a modest one-bedroom apartment in a once-and-not-yet-again-trendy neighborhood.

The savings had built up quickly, albeit not so quickly as her innate restlessness might have liked. And now ninety-five percent of those savings had been spent on a ship of her own.

Her ship.

She let *those* words roll around exquisitely in her mind as she went to break the good news to her boss.

SENECA

CAVARE, CAPITAL OF THE SENECAN FEDERATION

Caleb Marano flattened himself against the wall and readied the Daemon at his hip.

From the other side of the entrance Samuel counted down the seconds with his fingers. When the last finger dropped Samuel activated the door and they stormed into the room.

A makeshift office containing only a collapsible desk sitting askew and cartons stacked along both walls, the setting carried all the hallmarks of shady and transient criminal activity.

"Pascal Abelli, you are under arrest for blackmail and extortion of a government official. You may—"

"I don't think so." Abelli drew his own Daemon as footsteps pounded down the hallway behind them.

The investigation had fallen to the Division of Intelligence because there was some question as to whether a government official, Interior Director Orsi De Campo, had in truth engaged in the crime Abelli was blackmailing him to keep secret—selling Federation secrets to the Triene cartel. If the Director had not done so, the pertinent question became how classified material had found its way into Pascal Abelli's hands.

Samuel shot Abelli before the gun made it halfway up. Caleb stayed by the entrance, waited a beat, then threw an elbow backwards to smash the face of the guard who burst through the doorway, knocking the man flat on his back as blood gushed from a crushed nasal septum.

He spun and fired as the guard tried to get up, confiscated the man's gun and tossed it to Samuel. Next he crouched to search the now unconscious form for other weapons.

Laser fire streaked above his head. He lunged forward to tackle the second guard at the knees when the opposite wall turned red in a spray of blood propelled out of the hole burned through the man's chest. The body collapsed to the floor.

After Caleb checked to confirm the hallway harbored no further attackers, he climbed to his feet and found Samuel lowering the gun Caleb had tossed to him, his personal shield sparking with residual energy dissipation.

"Guess *his* gun wasn't set to stun. And I thought I might actually get to finish this op without having to kill anyone."

"When was the last time that happened?"

"Too long ago to remember, seems like." Samuel flipped Abelli's prone body onto his stomach and secured his arms in wrist restraints. "This guy's a lard-ass. Help me drag him out?"

Caleb wiped stray blood off his cheek using his shirt before grabbing hold of the unconscious man's left arm. Together they hauled him past the two guards and down the hallway.

"Thanks for tagging along with me tonight—turns out I did need the backup. Logistics ought to be here by the time we get outside. I'd invite you to go get a beer or four, but I suspect I'm going to be ass-deep in red tape for hours. Killing politicians, their friends or even their enemies always means mountains of bureaucracy."

A beer or four *would* serve well to calm the adrenaline still coursing hot through Caleb's veins and the agitated energy which inevitably lingered longer than it should after such confrontations.

But there was more than one way to appease the restlessness.

"It's all good. I've got plans on Romane later." 'Plans' was perhaps a strong word, but Samuel didn't need to know that. "Next time?"

Samuel grunted as they lugged Abelli around another corner. "Next time it is."

A

ERISEN

EARTH ALLIANCE COLONY

"Are you ready?"

"For fuck's sake, Ken, I've been waiting a month for the ship to be finished. I am beyond ready."

Kennedy Rossi rolled her eyes as they approached one of the hangar bays at IS Design's production facility. "I just don't want you to faint when you see it or anything."

"I've never fainted in my life. Why on Earth would I faint now?"

"Well…." Kennedy entered a code on the panel beside the interior bay entrance and let the door slide open.

Alex crossed the threshold, at which point all other thoughts vacated her mind as her perception narrowed, transfixed by the vision exposed before her.

The ship gleamed a charcoal two shades from black. All curves and edges, the broad midsection flared out to expansive wings which housed—or would soon house—a plethora of instruments and sensors. From an aesthetic viewpoint, the silhouette resembled an Indian Black Eagle preparing to swoop upon its prey.

Her gaze ran bow to stern and back again. Though a small vessel by any objective measure, here in the hangar it loomed large and powerful to dominate its environs.

"You're blocking the door, Alex."

"I know I'm blocking the door. Give me a minute."

She had to credit the engineers. She had provided them a design, and they had brought it to life more vividly than it had ever existed in her imagination. A grin spread across her face as she at last approached the ship.

"You would not believe how much grumbling I caught from, well, everyone on the project. 'Nobody makes ships like this,' 'We'll never fit slots for so many instruments on the frame,' 'I've never even heard of this material'…on and on it went."

Alex ignored her to run a hand along the hull, following it all the way to the sLume drive suspended beneath a gracefully tapered tail section. Though faster than eighty percent of civilian drives, it was a previous-generation model and the most she could afford right now.

Everything was designed with an affinity toward continual iterative transformation, though, and if all went according to plan she'd be able to upgrade it soon enough. This was the case for many of the on-board components: solid, quality last-gen equipment she intended would one day be replaced by the state of the art.

But the ship…the ship holding them was one of a kind.

She traced the hull to the hatch. Already keyed to her, it opened at her touch. She was vaguely cognizant of Kennedy trailing her up the ramp, then rather more cognizant of it when she halted at the top and Kennedy bumped into her and sent her skidding into the cabin.

She stood silently in the center of the cabin for several seconds…then she was laughing and twirling around in the cavernous open space like a carefree child. "Ken, *look*. This is amazing!"

Her best friend leaned against the cabin wall to watch the rare display of exuberance in amusement. "So it's what you wanted?"

"Well, I'll need to run diagnostics on the mechanical systems and confirm the HUD layout and test all the modules against my specs and I hope like hell the engineering core's wiring isn't a complete disaster…" she glanced at Kennedy to find her wearing a mock glare "…but yes. It's exactly what I wanted. It's—it's everything I wanted. Thank you."

"You are most welcome. But we hardly worked gratis. You paid my company bucket-loads of credits for it."

"True, but those bucket-loads were a scintilla above cost, so I'll double-down on the 'thank you.' I could not have commissioned this ship if it had included a retail markup."

"You've given the designers here some clever ideas to pursue. I predict we will soon recoup the initial loss in profit."

"Hmm." Alex scrutinized the main cabin once more before arching an eyebrow. "Want to go somewhere? Take her for a test run?"

Kennedy made a show of considering the question. "Only if we go somewhere with top-shelf shopping. I need new shoes. Lots of new shoes."

"Well I'm broke now, so I'll be a poor shopping partner."

"That's fine, I don't require an enabler. I'll do plenty of buying for both of us."

Alex pondered it a moment. "Romane?"

Kennedy's face lit up. "Romane."

ᴙ

ROMANE

INDEPENDENT COLONY

"Caleb, this is a surprise." Mia Requelme's lips curled up in an expression somewhere between delight and anticipation. "A pleasant one, naturally."

He placed a kiss at her temple then stepped a respectful distance away, as they had an audience. "How are you? It's been a few months."

"I'm good. I signed a lease last week on a new retail location. I'm expanding the store." She gestured at the cramped, cluttered space to emphasize the necessity of the act.

He wasn't surprised. It had taken her a few months to get her feet under her after arriving on Romane, but once she had it was off to the races. In less than five years she had gone from renting a cubbyhole behind a flat to a five-room apartment, from trading secondhand gear in the flea market to owning a custom tech shop in an upscale neighborhood. And he suspected she was barely getting started.

Mia checked the two customers browsing her shelves then leaned in close to murmur in his ear. "I'm devastated to say I can't leave for another five hours. I only have part-time help, and said help is currently on vacation."

He chuckled; she had obviously deduced why he was here. "Well, I don't—"

Mia's eyes darted to the entrance, her expression darkening. He turned to see what had distracted her.

A man hovered a step inside the store. His scruffy appearance and grungy clothes set him apart from not only the other customers but everyone in a six-block radius. They marked him as a thug.

Caleb demanded the entrant's attention with his eyes and held it hostage with a sharp, silent stare.

The man balked under the scrutiny. He glared at Mia and departed.

"So anyway—"

"What just happened?"

"Nothing. As I was saying—"

"Mia...."

She blew out an exasperated breath. "Don't worry about it. It's fine."

Now he demanded *her* attention, though in a far softer manner. "Are you in some kind of trouble?"

"Not at all. I can take care of myself."

"I know you can. So tell me what it was about."

She drew him to the rear wall of the shop, farther from her customers' hearing. "He's an enforcer for this upstart local gang. They've gotten it in their heads they're going to run a protection racket." She sighed in blatant disgust. "Even here, at the center of a pillar of our civilization, there are still goons and delinquents lurking in the shadows."

"Are you paying them?"

"No. But...."

"But?"

"I'm starting to think it may be better for me to simply do so and be done with it." Her gaze slid away as she shifted her weight from one leg to the other. Her arms crossed over her chest. "They're low-rent scum, but they have muscle. They've gotten violent against several of the more recalcitrant store owners. Two have ended up in the hospital, and...the last person who said 'no' more than twice ended up dead."

"Okay, that's it." He pivoted toward the door, but was halted by her hand grasping his wrist.

"Caleb, please don't. This isn't your fight. The police are investigating, and if they don't handle it, I will."

"Mia, this is what I *do*. Let me help you."

Dark irises glittered beneath long lashes pinched tight. The intensity of the look reminded him she was indeed a formidable woman. "You've already helped me enough for two lifetimes—given me the capability to live a life of my own—and I adore you for it. But you've done enough." She studied his face. "Do you hear me?"

He nodded with an air of thoughtfulness, careful to project the impression he was taking her words to heart. "I hear you. Just watch yourself, will you?"

She smiled broadly, breaking the somber mood. "Always."

He forced a devilish smirk. "So five hours, huh? All right, I'll make myself scarce." He drew her close and his lips found her ear. "I'll come by later tonight. You haven't moved your apartment, have you?"

"No, but who said I wanted you to come by tonight? Maybe I have a date."

"Then I'll come by *after* your date." His teeth grazed her neck as he pulled back to find a glint in her eyes he recognized as assent. With a casual wave he left her to her customers and headed out.

Kennedy's shopping bags were jammed under their patio table. Empty plates sat discarded to the side, a nearly-empty bottle of shiraz in the center. They took turns devouring an enormous slice of cheesecake drizzled in raspberries as the sky began darkening to a cool lavender. Romane's two suns made for a very long if most lovely evening.

"So what are your initial plans for this new venture?"

Alex enjoyed savoring her bite of cheesecake before answering. "I have an appointment first of the week with the R&D Director of Suiren about mining for nanodiamonds in NGC 2027, and one the next day with a rep from the Gagarin Institute about scouting M10 for potentially habitable worlds."

"You don't waste any time, do you?"

"Hell, no. I've been preparing for this opportunity my whole life. I am ready to get on with it."

"And you won't get lonely, out there by yourself in the void for weeks at a stretch? Wait, what am I saying? This is you we're talking about." She paused to take another bite and wipe away the raspberry sauce left behind on her chin. "So did you tell your mother you left Pacifica to go freelance?"

Alex scowled over the top of her glass of shiraz. "As if she would care. She's a newly-minted Admiral and on the shortlist to be the next EASC Director of Operations."

"So…?"

"*Yes*, I sent her a message. In vintage Miriam Solovy fashion, she responded that she hoped I understood I bore the responsibility for my own foolish choices."

"Well…nope, sorry, can't defend her on this one. You've worked your ass off for four years—for a decade if you count earning multiple degrees—so you could make your dream a reality. She should respect what you've accomplished."

Alex didn't dispute the truth of the statement, though she did swallow a brief disquiet when Kennedy paid the check. She'd feel bad about it, except for the fact that while she wasn't quite 'broke' by the most technical definition, the ship had eradicated her savings. And she didn't have a proper job. Or any clients. Not yet.

So she decided not to feel bad about it. She and Kennedy had traded implicit debts which never needed to be repaid yet always were more times than she dared count over the years. This debt too was sure to come back around again eventually.

R

The instant Caleb exited Mia's store his demeanor transformed. He traded the relaxed gait for a careful, alert posture and the friendly countenance for a cool mask.

It did not surprise him to see the enforcer exit a store three doors down a moment later. The man was making his scheduled rounds. When his target continued on he followed.

The sidewalk ferried a busy flow of young professionals out after work and tourists perusing the shops and restaurants. The thug's distinctly unkempt appearance made him easy to track from a distance.

A line spilled out of a particularly popular Chinasian grill restaurant on the next corner. An expansive outdoor patio decorated in wrought iron and blooming alyssi blended into an open-air interior, and the place bustled with energy. In another circumstance he'd likely have wandered inside for stir-fry and a cold beer.

As he slipped past the busy entrance someone tripped into him. He stiffened, keeping the stranger at a safe distance until he realized the person was merely inebriated beyond public decency. He tried to stabilize the young man, but his efforts were for naught when the guy stumbled to the ground.

Caleb stepped away to avoid the prone figure and immediately bumped into someone else. Golden curls whipped past him as he muttered, "Excuse me."

"Not a problem."

At the sound of the rich, almost sultry voice he instinctively glanced back. The golden curls belonged to an attractive, poised young woman and were promptly forgotten when beyond her he caught a glimpse of tresses the color of fine Bordeaux and a flash of startlingly bright silver-gray eyes.

The sight was enough to hitch his gait for half a step, to overwhelm his mission for a frozen frame of time.

Then she was gone, and he resumed his tail.

Æ

The waitress cleared away the dessert plates and Kennedy gathered her bags up. Alex frowned as they wound into the restaurant from the patio and navigated a growing crowd near the exit. "You seriously need to be on Erisen by first thing in the morning?"

"I do. I have to work. You've been job-free for all of a day, surely you remember what 'working' means?"

"*Sosi yego i past' zakroi, suka.*"

"Right, right."

"Next thing I know you're going to want to sleep in the big bed. First night on my shiny, brand new ship and I'm bunking on the guest cot."

"Now that you mention it, I do need to be well-rested and refreshed for work in the morn—" Kennedy jostled into Alex's side, pushed by someone bumping into her as they exited the busy doorway.

"Excuse me." The deep, lilting voice resonated beneath the buzz of the patrons, sending a sensual tremor fluttering along Alex's spine. Taken aback by the unexpected, visceral response, she blinked and forcibly shook it off.

"Not a problem." Kennedy's focus lingered over her shoulder as they reached the sidewalk. "He was handsome, in a rugged, 'rock my world for a weekend' sort of way."

"Whatever. Come on, there's a tech gear shop on the next block I want to check out."

"I thought you were broke?"

"This is why they invented credit. I'm investing in my ship."

"Clearly. Speaking of, have you decided what you're going to name her?"

A whimsical smile grew to brighten Alex's features as they strolled down the sidewalk in the slowly fading light. "Oh yes."

Several blocks past the restaurant the ambience of the area began to shift. Meter by meter it became shabbier, darkening in sync with the evening sky. The crowd thinned and was replaced by working-class then barely working-class inhabitants. Finally Caleb's opportunity came.

He increased his pace to draw near to his prey. As the enforcer crossed an alley between two shabby tenements he sprang, forcing the man down the alley, deep into the shadows and far from prying bystanders, and shoving his head into the stone.

Yanking the right arm up at an awkward angle flush against the man's back, he held it at the end of its range of motion for a beat then thrust it upward from the elbow.

The man screamed in pain as the bone ripped out of the elbow and shoulder sockets and the tendons tore apart.

The other arm flailed at Caleb; he pinned it high on the wall, knifed his hand and slammed it forward. The *crack* was audible as the man's forearm fractured under the blow.

In the next motion he wrenched his captive around and got in his face. "You are going to take me to the leaders of your little 'gang' and you are going to do it now."

Beads of sweat drizzled down greasy skin, doubtless triggered by what must be fairly intense pain if not fear. "I can't—"

"Don't talk. Don't sputter out a solitary protest or it will be your last. Take me to them."

"Who the fuck *are* you?"

Caleb palmed the man's forehead and slammed his skull against the wall. "I *said* don't talk, and you want to do as I say because I'm the one thing monsters like you and your kind fear. I'm what haunts your nightmares and hunts you in the darkness. Now *move*."

The man's head jerked wildly, slinging greasy sweat in Caleb's direction. He wiped the fluid off his chin then grabbed the arm flopping limply at his captive's side and pointed to the street.

Their destination lay a few short blocks further to the west, which was probably for the best because his charge was not holding up well. He groaned and moaned and eventually begged for Caleb to punch him hard enough to render him unconscious. Caleb kept driving him forward.

When they stepped through the door to the hideout he tossed his captive to the side and drew his Daemon.

Three men sat around a table. All were muscled and similarly greasy and easily identifiable as scum. As he breached the entrance all three were moving, drawing their own guns in surprise.

Only one got off a shot. Caleb had put a laser through the skulls of the other two before their arms had fully raised.

The third man wore a minimal personal shield and weathered Caleb's first volley to return fire.

The shots bounced harmlessly off his own shield. He advanced while firing into the gangster's chest. The laser overloaded the cheap shield to blow the man's chest open.

Ozone permeated the air to scorch his nostrils. He stood silently in the center of the room and allowed the scene to settle to its conclusion.

The body collapsed to the floor to join its companions, leaving the far wall free to reveal its gory tableau. The sound of glass cracking followed the thud of the corpse. A display panel on the desk behind the bodies, grazed by the gunfire, teetered and fell.

Another breath…in and out…and he was moving. After checking for immediate threats he went over to where the panel had landed.

A visual flickered, distorted in the damaged display, but he discerned a woman and a small boy. The woman was pretty in a mildly trashy way, sporting a crooked grin and too-blonde hair. The boy looked three or four and clearly favored his mother.

All the adrenaline abandoned him in a rush, leaving his shoulders sagging and the gun dangling from his hand.

They were thugs and bullies and murderers. They preyed on the weak and stole from those who worked rather than work themselves. They used fear as a weapon to impose their will on others. And they had pointed guns at him.

Yet a traitorous voice in his mind whispered that he had provoked the encounter; he had stormed into their lair, gun drawn. Yes, they would have killed him, but in the present situation perhaps only because he would have done—and did—the same to them.

Caleb didn't know which of the dead men the woman was attached to or which might be the father of the boy. For an instant it was the only question that mattered.

He snatched the display off the floor, spun on a heel and strode to the enforcer who had brought him here, now sprawled in a pile on the floor. He crouched and nudged him onto his back without a response. The man had passed out. Annoyed, Caleb slapped him awake.

As soon as an eyelid opened he grabbed the man's shirt and lifted him up to shove the display in his face. "Do you know this woman?"

He nodded vaguely, eyes bleary and unfocused.

"What is her name?"

"Tam—Tamatha Baker."

Caleb buried the tumult he had briefly allowed to flare, and his bearing took on an uncanny stillness. He smiled.

"This is your lucky day. You get to live—on one condition, so listen carefully. Your sole purpose from this day forward is to watch over Tamatha and her son and make certain neither of them come to harm. Use your meager, pathetic skills to protect them. Do you understand me?"

The man's eyes widened until they were all whites. A bead of sweat rolled down his forehead and merged with a trickle of blood to weave down his cheek and splatter onto his shirt. He nodded again, more definitively this time.

"If you fail in this task I will know, and I will come back and end your life as effortlessly as I ended theirs. Remember that whenever you start thinking you can slack off." He stared at the man another second to guarantee the message had been received, then dropped him to the floor and stood. "I'll send the paramedics and the cops in a few minutes. Make sure you don't get yourself arrested—can't do your job from prison."

"Why? Why did you kill them?"

Caleb laughed, and even he recognized it bore a frightening coldness. "Because you walked through the wrong door, and they paid you to do it. Mia Requelme is *off limits*. You will be a testament to the terror that arrives the moment you or anyone else crosses the invisible line you didn't know existed until tonight. Spread the word."

ℛ

ERISEN

EARTH ALLIANCE COLONY

The *Siyane* banked to soar above snow-capped mountains as the dawn sun glittered off the powdery crystals. The sky shone a perfect turquoise blue.

Alex had deposited Kennedy at the spaceport moments earlier, somewhat less refreshed and well-rested than requested. But it had been an enjoyable night. She stifled a yawn as she gained altitude and approached the nearest atmosphere corridor, but a smile replaced it. A couple of minutes remained for her to decide her destination once she hit space.

It was a subversive notion, the idea that she was free. Free to choose where to go and what to do with her time.

She wasn't a goldbricker. She intended to run a business and had crucial appointments the next week she intended to keep.

But at the conclusion of those appointments she would choose to take the jobs or not. If she took the jobs she would choose how best to fulfill the contracts. The path between the agreement and the delivery was hers to chart. She would succeed or fail on her own merits; her rise or fall would be of her own making.

Until then she had six days to herself, nothing but her ship and the expanse of space to distract her.

The ship exited the atmosphere corridor. The sky darkened to onyx and the stars brightened to opalescent ivory. Her father's words from so long ago echoed in her mind.

Siyane is perfect, sweetheart. My little star shining brightly. One day, milaya, the cosmos will be yours to tame. One day you will hold the galaxy in the palm of your hand. I know it.

She killed the lights in the cabin and stood to take in the view as the fullness of space spread before her.

Her head tilted in contemplation. Could she make it to Carina and get back to Earth in six days? She double-checked the parameters on the sLume drive...yep, she absolutely could. Six days round-trip for a spectacular view? Worth it.

Now clear of Erisen Traffic Control, she ran a quick safety check then engaged the sLume drive. The stars blurred away to surround the ship in a soft halo.

Hey Dad? I made it. I made it to the stars.

SOLATIUM

SOLATIUM

AN
AURORA
RHAPSODY

_AR_

SHORT STORY

G. S. JENNSEN

Morality could not be spawned by tweaking a few genes or shutting off a few neurons. Though humanity conquered the very stars, it remained unable to conquer the darkness within.

In the dark, seedy underbelly of Pandora—a lawless colony on the best of days—a young woman who's lost everything but her soul fights to reclaim her life from a violent, sadistic criminal despot. But when she's given a chance for freedom, she realizes escape is not enough. First, a just punishment must be exacted for crimes committed.

Set twelve years before *STARSHINE: Aurora Rising Book One (Amaranthe #1)*, *Solatium* is Mia Requelme's origin story—and the story of how she and Caleb Marano met. It's a story about criminals and those who punish them, but mostly it's a story about the struggle to keep hold of one's soul in the face of so much darkness.

*

Solatium is the story of how Mia and Caleb first met. It's also a buddy-action tale that gives a peek into Caleb's relationship with his former mentor, Samuel. But above all else, it's Mia's origin story. And she has one hell of an origin story!

Solatium is best read after you've read Starshine *at a minimum, so you have a sense of who Mia is now, but it works as a standalone story as well.*

DRAMATIS PERSONAE

Mia Requelme
Hacker, thief.
Faction: *Independent*

Caleb Marano
Special Operations intelligence agent,
Senecan Federation Division of Intelligence.
Faction: *Senecan Federation*

Samuel Padova
Special Ops, SF Intelligence;
mentor of Caleb Marano.
Faction: *Senecan Federation*

Eli Baca
Underworld crime boss.
Faction: *Independent*

"Vengeance is in my heart, death in my hand,
Blood and revenge are hammering in my head."

— William Shakespeare, Titus Andronicus

2310
(12 Years Before the Events of Starshine)

PANDORA

Independent Colony
North-Central Quadrant of Settled Space

The relentless thrum of hard synth spilling out of the dance club down the block set the fine hairs of Mia's forearm on edge. She pressed the fingertips of her left hand onto the door lock. Her glyphs lit up to send a burnished chrome ribbon swirling from the base of her neck down her arm to the pads of her fingers.

The glyphs seemed to fall into sync with the beat of the music, adopting the tempo the driving cadence demanded.

The door slid open and she slid through it.

It was pitch black inside the shop. She would kill for a decent infrared upgrade for her ocular implant, but paying for the single, solitary glyph stream had left her without a credit to her name, and now it was costing her credits she didn't have. Worth it.

She did have the floorplan stored in her eVi, however. She projected it to a tiny aural twelve centimeters in front of her face and felt along the walls in the dark until she located the business office.

The office door was locked as well, but it was a pitiful effort, and she was inside in seconds. Once the door closed she activated the lights, confident the office was far enough back for the light not to be seen from the street, then went straight to the desk.

The encryption on the control panel would be too robust for the internal hacking routines she kept stored in her eVi. She removed a small device from the pouch at her hip, connected it to the input port recessed in the desk's surface, switched on the screen and went to work.

⋀

Mia spared one sidelong glance at the dance club on her way out. Though she could see the strobes flash above the street and feel the rhythm of the music vibrating in her bones, the club couldn't be any more out of her reach if it were parsecs distant. It belonged to a world she'd never seen—a world of shimmery synthetic silks, exotic cybernetic enhancements and personal starships. It belonged to people who were free.

Seeing as she was not, she pivoted and went in the other direction, toward the levtram station. She needed to get the files she'd stolen to Eli.

Not that Eli would comprehend anything on the disk. He'd pass it on to his boss, who would pass it on to their boss and so on until it landed on the desk of Aiden Trieneri, 2.4 kiloparsecs away on New Babel. She hadn't been told why the files were desired, but they had included details on supply contracts and bank account transfers, several involving black market companies. So in her informed opinion, the head of the Triene criminal cartel wanted to blackmail the executives of Escapes Extraordinaire, probably for hundreds of thousands if not millions of credits.

Whereas she simply needed twenty credits. They would buy dim sum and noodles at Sumi's Cantonese House, with enough left over to pay for a ten-minute shower rental at the community center. Her stomach churned to remind her how long it had been since she'd eaten.

Yesterday morning, it grumbled in an accusatory tone.

There was a bread roll last night, she grumbled in retort.

Oh, god, she was conversing with her stomach like it had sentience. She was going mad, and without even a chimeral addiction to blame for it. She had to get out of this nightmarish prison her life had become.…

"Give a guy a hit, doll?"

She recoiled in disgust at the filth pawing at her arm. Oily, stringy hair hung in clumps around a gaunt face. His tongue flicked out at her from between cracked, bleeding lips.

Her hand swept out to knock him to the ground. "I don't have what you're hunting for, trust me."

As Mia whipped away, something incongruous flitted in the edge of her vision. She continued walking and didn't alter her demeanor while she scanned the area. Was someone following her? She casually checked over her shoulder, but saw nothing—nothing beyond the trippers and the drunks, the peddlers and the pawns.

Maybe she was getting too paranoid; maybe it came with the madness. She shook off the apprehension. She'd almost reached her destination, anyway. Eli's hangout sat right in the heart of slum central.

Chimerals were available everywhere on Pandora. Hell, the colony was effectively one big party planet. But there were two kinds of drug-seekers who resorted to frequenting the neighborhood known as The Channel: those who could only afford the cheap, dangerous chimerals, and those who used to be able to afford the quality stuff, had gotten addicted, had gotten poor and now could only afford the cheap, dangerous chimerals.

She instinctively held her breath as she entered the 'lounge' where Eli spent many of his late night hours. Aside from the smell of too much stale sweat, Eli piped Surf through the ventilation system—the act of walking inside got you high, so gradually you didn't realize it. He did it so his customers would be more relaxed and less inclined to haggle over price or product. He'd built up an immunity to it long ago. She'd written her own routine for her eVi to filter the chemical out of her bloodstream as fast as possible, but she still felt sick whenever she was inside.

The bouncer grunted upon recognizing her and let her pass into the main room. In the smoky, wavering light it looked the same as it always did. Trippers lined the walls, sampling merchandise from the teaser dispensers while Eli's muscle watched them, ready to toss anyone who got too greedy.

Eli was sprawled on a couch in the middle of the room. Corpulent and greasy, his belly overhung atrocious fuchsia leather pants. A ripped, sleeveless shirt showed off glowing scarlet tattoos down both arms—they looked like glyphs, but they were fake. He wouldn't know a self-directed cybernetics routine if it crawled up in his head and transformed him into a dancing monkey. She snickered to herself at the image; what if one already had?

He was finishing up a business transaction as she approached. At his nod, one of his guys off to the side offered a square box to the customer.

"…works out, there will be crates of this waiting for you."

The man turned to leave, throwing her a leer when he passed her. She ignored him to thrust the data disk from Escapes Extraordinaire toward Eli.

"I got your files. Didn't run into any problems. Now pay me."

He made a face at the disk and waved her off. "Go take it to Isaiah. He'll get it on a transport. I'll pay you when he says the data's good."

Annoyance and hunger gnawed at her gut. "Fuck, Eli—I'm not one of your pansy runners!"

His hand shot out and grabbed her wrist, yanking her onto her knees in front of him. "You're whatever I say you are, sweetie, because I *own* you. Don't I?"

Spit gathered on her tongue, ready to spew forth. Hit him between the eyes with it. She could do it.

"Say it!" His meaty, clammy fingers tightened their grip until they cut off the blood flow to her hand.

She swallowed the spit, and the last vestiges of her imagined dignity accompanied it down her throat. The whisper escaped through gritted teeth. "You own me."

"That's better." He let go with a forceful shove to send her sprawling onto her ass. "Now do as you're told and take the disk to Isaiah."

"Yes, *sir*." Hatred seethed in her glare as she crawled to her feet...but he had turned his back on her to gesture at the bartender for a drink.

She stalked toward the door, acidic self-loathing rising up to burn her chest, so when another hand grabbed her bruised and aching wrist, she kneed the assaulter in the ribs.

"Dammit, Mia!" Paul clutched at his side with a moan. "What'd you do that for?"

"General principle," she muttered and resumed course for the door.

"Hey, wait—" he managed to regain a slight hold on her and dragged her into the supply alcove, then blocked her exit "—we need to have a conversation."

"Not now, Paul. I've got places to be." She tore her wrist out of his grasp. She wanted to massage it but didn't dare lose yet more face with yet more people who held power over her.

"I think you owe me some credits before you go."

She sighed heavily as a flood of weariness—the existential kind sleep could never heal—overwhelmed her. "He hasn't paid me yet, okay? Never mind that I'm the best hacker he's got. I also have to be one of his bitch runners and ferry a delivery to the boss."

"Javier's as good a hacker as you."

"No, he's not. You know how I know he's not? Eli put him in the hospital last week for buggering up a job on Galaxy First. Eli hasn't put me in the hospital." He'd come close a few times, but she kept this detail to herself.

Paul's jaw dropped for a beat until he recovered a measure of false bravado. "Javier's sloppy—but so are you. I mean, I caught you at your dirty dealing, didn't I?" He grabbed her by the hair and pinned her against the wall. "You make sure and send me my cut of your pay by sunrise, or I'll rat you out to Eli. I'll tell him you were skimming off your jobs, and he will slice your skinny neck open from ear to ear."

"Cause you're too chicken-shit to do it yourself." She kneed him again, lower this time, gathered her hair back into its tail and stepped over his writhing body. "You'll get your money, like you always do."

She made it half a block before doubling-over and retching from the nausea—of the poisoned air inside, of her body's attempts to save her from its ill effects, of her conscience's disgust at the evening's events. Or maybe it was the fear. It was only dry heaves, though. She hadn't eaten in twenty hours.

After a few slow inhales she straightened up and considered the long gauntlet of The Channel. Isaiah's place was up in the far, far nicer Promenade, where proper criminals did proper business. She had a long way to go.

If only she could keep going. Further, until there were stars ahead of her.

There must be another way, a better way, of living. Glimpses of it teased her in the spaceport and on the exanet and at the synth dance clubs parsecs away down the street.

She simply needed a chance to grab hold of it. One real chance.

"She's the one."

Samuel eyed Caleb skeptically as they tailed the young woman through a side thoroughfare of The Boulevard. "I know what you're thinking, but she's too young for you."

"No, she's too young for *you*, old man—and just because you're thinking it, doesn't mean I am. She's the right choice."

The woman had stopped to browse at a kiosk, and they did the same. Samuel picked up a neon lime t-shirt featuring an animated character painted on the front and held it out to inspect it. "All right. Tell me why."

Caleb squelched a rude reply. Almost four years had passed since he'd been Samuel's trainee; they were on this mission as equals. Technically. Yet he found himself answering as if he were still the student. "Watch how she moves. She's cognizant of everyone around her—where they are, where they're heading. Her eyes scan a crowd the way ours do—seeing it all and each tiny detail. This one's smart, quick and self-aware."

"That means she's a talented thief. It doesn't mean you can turn her."

He grimaced when Samuel held the t-shirt to his chest, shaking his head in firm disapproval. "I've seen her interact with Eli's people. If looks could kill, there'd be a string of bodies leading all the way from here to Eli's door. She thinks she's better than them, and she's not wrong. But she's also malnourished and essentially homeless, which means she doesn't have a way out."

"And you're going to give her one, be a big goddamn hero."

He frowned, taken aback by the cynical tone with which the statement was delivered. Not because Samuel wasn't often cynical—he was—but because Caleb had assumed that was the goal. "Well...yes. If she gives us the access codes to Eli's manufacturing facility, it's just compensation."

"True." Samuel folded the t-shirt and returned it to the table as up ahead the woman began moving again. After a suitable delay, they followed. "Sure you don't want to grab one of Eli's underlings and beat them until they spill their guts?"

He regarded his partner, deadpan. The man didn't enjoy roughing up people, even thugs, any more than he did. Not much more than he did.

Samuel groused and rubbed at his beard. "It was only a suggestion. If you say she's the one, make your play. I've got your back."

"Why should I help you?" the woman snarled at Caleb like some kind of feral cat.

He'd intercepted her as she pilfered a stack of disks from a merchant kiosk and escorted her to an alley off The Boulevard thoroughfare, then launched into his pitch. "Because I can get you out. I'll even get you off-planet, to somewhere you can start a new life."

"I already started a new life once. Didn't help."

Caleb smiled at her. It was genuine...and also happened to be part of the soft sell. "But I bet you have a list a kilometer long of the mistakes you made and how you would get it right the next time. Help me, and let me help you find your next time."

Her eyes narrowed warily to scrutinize him. He let her, refusing to wilt under her admittedly impressive stare, but also not bristling in challenge. He could see the thoughts race behind her dark irises, see her weighing the pros and cons of hearing him out...but when the scales didn't tip in his favor after several seconds, he decided it was time to sweeten the deal.

"I tell you what. Why don't you let me buy you some dinner, and you can think it over while we're eating."

She scowled and ran a hand through tangled, dirty hair, and he knew he had her. "Fine. It's your money."

He gestured toward the alley exit and silently pulsed Samuel.

We're on the move. Burrito joint we passed farther up The Boulevard.

I'll follow dutifully behind and watch your ass.

She ate for five solid minutes before pausing long enough to talk to him, having devoured half the giant burrito with the gusto of a last meal.

"What are you planning to do to Eli's operation?"

Eli Baca might be a degenerate, but he ran an increasingly high-volume chimeral production business. Not of the light, non-addictive drugs that fueled raves and *illusoire* parties, either. He was manufacturing hard chimerals, the type that stood a reasonable chance of burning out the user's brain on any given hit.

Competition in the drug trade was fierce here on Pandora, but it was far less so across the Senecan Federation border on the small colonies of Caelum, Bellici and Palluda. When Eli started shipping his product across the border, it became the business of the Federation's Division of Intelligence—which meant it became Caleb and Samuel's business.

Strictly speaking, Division didn't have jurisdiction to act on Pandora's soil, since it was not a Federation colony. But Pandora had no government to speak of, thus no one had jurisdiction to act there. Thus everyone had jurisdiction.

"I'm going to explosively dismantle his chimeral production line and bring the cops down on the remains."

"There aren't any cops here."

He laughed. "Yes, there are."

"Well, could've fooled me." She took another bite, stuffing her mouth full of rice, beans and olives, and regarded him over the burrito. Food in her stomach had emboldened her, and he began to feel legitimate heat from her probing eyes.

One of Eli's enforcers just spotted you two. I'll take care of him.
He didn't outwardly react to Samuel's pulse.

We're sitting here having dinner. He shouldn't be suspicious.

Unless he's smart. Unlikely, but in case, I'll take care of him.

"Why would you help me?"

Of course she was mistrustful and wary. Everyone around her was using her for their own ends. He wondered if anyone had ever looked out for her.

"Because you're a better person than they are. You're intelligent and quick and you clearly have skills. I can see the potential beneath the grime."

Are you seriously using that line again?

Shut up. It's true.

It's still a line.

Aren't you supposed to be handling some goon?

Handled.

Caleb shifted his posture subtly to lean in closer. "Besides, you don't like what you're doing. You don't like being a criminal, and you definitely don't like being beholden to a scumbag like Eli."

"How could you possibly tell all that about me? You just met me."

A corner of his mouth curled up in a smirk. "I've been watching you for a few days and—"

"Impossible. I pay very close attention—I'd realize if I were being followed."

"Yes, you do. But I'm better than you."

She snorted and finished off the burrito.

Goon might have called in reinforcements before being handled. 'Might have'?

Did. I've got a solid bead on one, but if the other makes it past me you'll have to deal with him.

Then don't fucking let him get past you. This woman's apt to rabbit on me if I so much as cough wrong.

He took a sip of water and scanned the crowd. "As I was saying. I've been watching you, along with several other of Eli's lackeys. I need someone on the inside, and it was simply a matter of deciding who. I chose you. Did I make the wrong choice?"

She finished off the chips next and sank back in her chair to study him in silence again. It took all his self-control to meet her gaze calmly and not jerk his eyes around in search of the attack that threatened to arrive any minute.

"How do I know you won't double-cross me?"

Caleb reached in his pocket and pulled out a small translucent film. He laid it on the table but kept two fingers securely atop it. "Here's a ticket to Romane. Give me the access codes, I give you the ticket and transfer two thousand credits to you. You can leave right away."

Also handled. I'm bleeding, but it's fine, really. Take your time.

He had her full and undivided attention now and didn't dare divide his own to respond to Samuel.

She tilted her head at him. "How do you know I won't double-cross *you* and give you the wrong codes?"

His shoulders rose a fraction. He'd wrangled a first name out of her on the walk over. Names were powerful—which was why he'd given her a false one—and this was the time to use it. "I guess I'll have to trust you. Are you worthy of my trust, Mia?"

She stared at him a moment…and nodded.

ℛ

Mia focused on walking in a direction that would take her to the spaceport. She didn't focus on the ticket in her pocket. She didn't focus on the impossible two thousand credits in her bank account, already deposited mere seconds after she'd departed the restaurant.

She didn't need to focus on getting her belongings; she didn't have any. Well, she had two changes of clothes in a pack she stowed in the closet of a shop run by one of the few people she sort of trusted, but she didn't plan to retrieve them. She'd buy new clothes when she arrived on Romane, because she had *two thousand* credits.

Get a grip on yourself, Mia. You have to make the money last. This is your one real chance, and you better not screw it up. She took a deep breath and began to plan. She should—

—In the corner of her vision Fletch Godan, one of Eli's enforcers, crossed the intersection to her left. Was he after her? Did they know somehow? It seemed absurd, but Eli would stop at nothing to keep hold of her. He'd never willingly let her go. He needed her, but more relevantly, he never surrendered anything for which he claimed ownership.

What if this Federation 'intelligence agent'—he'd said his name was Josh—failed? What if Eli's people killed him in the assault? Worse, what if they captured him and he gave her up rather than suffer the unspeakable torture Eli would gleefully subject him to?

He was too damn attractive to be good at his job, anyway. That devilish smirk and those twinkling sapphire eyes of his were not going to be sufficient to take Eli out, much less a block-sized building of armed thugs.

She slipped into a grocery to get off the street and pretended to browse the aisles while she worked through her options.

If she departed Pandora without confirming Eli was dead, she'd live the rest of her days in fear, always peering over her shoulder, searching for ghosts in the shadows.

But if she stayed and Eli survived, she'd never get away...unless she took advantage of the chaos and managed to kill him herself. Not that she had a gun. Or a blade. Though if she could get her hands on a blade, she knew how to use one. She'd done it before....

"Excuse me, can I help you find something?"

Mia blinked out of the reverie to find the store clerk regarding her expectantly. "No, thank you." She spun and left the grocery before the clerk accused her of trying to steal something. Little did he know, if she were to try she'd succeed.

She'd spent the first year after fleeing to Pandora petrified the man she'd stabbed in a dim alley on New Orient hadn't died and was going to show up and kill her. Or her father was going to show up and kill her, or her brother. The fear had faded in time, but while under its influence she'd done stupid things, made poor decisions—decisions that ultimately resulted in her indentured servitude to Eli. She couldn't make the same mistakes again.

She felt certain this Josh guy wouldn't move on Eli's place until after night fell. This meant she had a few hours. Which was fortunate, because she needed to buy a blade and a coat.

The industrial district presented a starkly different picture from the rest of Pandora's public spheres. Gone were the bright lights, multi-sensory ads and constant, raucous music. In their place was street after street of drab, unadorned and unmarked buildings: warehouses, factories, plants and loading docks.

The night sky gleamed a faint dusty rose under heavy cloud-cover, and the dampness of the air signaled imminent rain. It was the perfect night and the perfect setting for their mission.

It would be easy to assume this was a criminal ward and every structure hid nefarious deeds, but that would be an error. Perhaps a quarter of the enterprises engaged in gray market or black market trade or outright illegal activity, but the remainder serviced the engine of Pandora's entertainment economy in a legal manner.

Eli Baca's enterprise fit squarely in the 'nefarious' category, however, churning out a variety of chimerals that weren't merely illegal, but dangerous and often deadly. They were supplied to a cross-colony underclass who preferred to spend their meager credits on another hit rather than the medical treatment guaranteed to save them. This style of business could never be completely stamped out. There would always be an underclass, and it would always include people for whom physical and mental pleasure was the beginning and end of their ambition.

Didn't mean Caleb didn't take great joy in trying, though. He checked his pack and the weapons on his belt a final time while Samuel did the same.

"Wish we could carry more explosives. It's a big building."

He nodded in nominal agreement and activated his personal concealment and defense shields. "More weighs us down too much. We'll just have to place them appropriately."

Samuel chuckled under his breath. "That we can do. Ready?"

"Always." Caleb unlatched his Daemon from his belt and exited the alley.

Eli's facility was located three blocks in, past a food service broker and two textile packagers. They planned to infiltrate the structure from the rear, incapacitate anyone they encountered, place remote detonation charges at strategic locations throughout the building, exit out the front door and blow the place.

It was Caleb's hope Eli would be onsite and suffer the same fate as his facility, but his attendance wasn't required. The complete destruction of his equipment and assembly lines should put the man in a sufficiently weakened position to ensure an ambitious competitor or subordinate took him out before he could rebuild. Conversely, taking out Eli alone wasn't enough. Someone would take his place in a matter of days.

They moved swiftly and quietly, staying close to the building façades and in the shadows. The concealment shields didn't provide complete invisibility, but in such a poorly lit area they came close, and the near infrared mode in their ocular implants allowed them to see as clearly as if it were daytime.

Two armed guards stood watch outside the rear entrance to the facility. If they got off an alarm, the rest of the mission became decidedly more difficult. Single headshots would eliminate them—if they weren't wearing personal shields. But why wouldn't they be?

He pulsed Samuel so as not to risk any noise.

I think we have to waste one of our charges.

Starting the night with an explosion won't exactly help the subterfuge.

I'm not going to detonate it—I'm going to throw it.

Ah. Pity to waste it, but…yeah. Go for it.

He retrieved a charge from his pack, counted down with his fingers, leaned out past the wall and hurled it high above the guards' heads into the next intersection.

The loud clang as it impacted a wall, the street then another wall immediately drew their attention. They jerked to alert, spun toward the sound and cautiously approached the source.

Caleb sprinted forward, confident his partner followed a step after him. He reached the first guard the same instant the man became aware of movement and started to shift around. He grappled the guard from behind and slammed one hand over the man's mouth as the other thrust a blade into his throat. The man struggled in his clutches, but it was a struggle of panic rather than directed intent.

The guard went limp; he eased the body to the ground and dragged it down the sidewalk and around the corner. Samuel appeared hauling the other body, and they stowed them in an alcove. There wasn't much pedestrian traffic in this district, so it was possible they wouldn't be found for…actually ever, since the exploding structure was going to take the bodies out with it.

Much of the blood from the neck wound had been absorbed into the guard's tactical clothing, but Caleb's hand was nonetheless coated in it. He wiped his palm on his pants since he didn't want a slick grip, but bloodstains were part of the job.

They headed back to the entrance. From this point forward, time was their enemy as much as the people inside.

Two massive, reinforced doors still stood between them and the interior.

Time to see if I wasted two thousand credits.

Caleb carefully input the complex series of access codes Mia had provided—one mistake and the alarm would sound, alerting everyone in a kilometer radius to their presence—then waited. Seconds ticked by.

The light beside the doors flipped to green.

See? I told you she was the right one.

You are such a softie.

An additional code was required to get them inside the offices up front, but he was now confident it would work as well.

Through the doors they entered a storage room. Crates lined the walls up to the ceiling…finished product ready to be shipped.

Looks like an excellent place for a detonation to me.

Samuel attached one of the charges to the side of a crate, hidden near the wall. A single charge would obliterate this room and those it abutted—a solid start, but it represented a fraction of the damage they hoped to do.

The hall outside led to a row of supply rooms where individual components were stored until needed. They startled a tech in the third room and neutralized her before she managed to scream.

Caleb acknowledged the twinge of remorse that always accompanied these types of kills. Not everyone who worked in the building bore as much guilt as Eli; while they weren't lily-white innocents, many were surely just trying to get by in life. Some were probably trapped as deeply as Mia. But he had no time to stop and ask each person he met which one they were, and they all knew the risks of working for someone like Eli.

The bulk of the interior consisted of a series of discrete assembly lines housed in individual rooms that ran nearly the length of the building. This worked to their advantage: they could place charges in the corridors between each room and didn't need to breach the rooms themselves. Muted but steady sounds leaking through the walls indicated the lines continued to operate despite the lateness of the hour. Though some of the assembly process was doubtless automated, any entry would still be a bloodbath. The people inside were going to die in the end either way, but this way they'd never know what happened.

They reached the doors to the office space with a minimum of interruptions, all of which were dispatched with a minimum of difficulty.

Caleb input the additional code, smiling to himself when this light also flipped to green, and flattened himself against the wall opposite Samuel. Anyone they encountered from here on out was certain to be armed.

How many charges left?

Two. You?

Same.

It's enough. One for Eli's office, one for the server room and the rest wherever we can.

They had barely entered the first hallway when voices wafted around the corner. Exposed and seeing nowhere to hide, they sprinted to close the distance. Ten meters still remained when two men rounded the corner. Shock registered on their faces, but these were trained guards and both had Daemons raised in less than a second.

Laser fire erupted as Caleb plowed into them, his arms spread wide to knock them to the floor with him. The energy from the lasers hissed and sparked on his shield.

He slammed his forearm into the wrist of the man on the left, sending a gun skittering across the floor. The other guard began to rise up beside him—

—and collapsed onto his back, Samuel's blade buried in his forehead to the hilt.

The man beneath him persisted in struggling, finally landing an uppercut on Caleb's chin that sent his head snapping sideways. He thrust his own blade up and into the man's abdomen under his tactical vest.

"Fu—!" He brought his other hand to his jaw and tried to blink past the jarring pain. It came away streaked in blood from a busted lip.

He glanced at the other body and climbed to his feet.

You threw your blade at him? Really?

Samuel shrugged dramatically.

It worked, didn't it? I have skills.

The racket generated by the melee would have drawn notice, and soon the sound of pounding feet and muffled yells filled the air.

Time to wrap this show up.

Yep.

Caleb punched a charge onto the wall and moved forward.

A few haphazard shots deterred two pursuers while Samuel tossed another charge through the open door of the server room, then they sprinted in the direction of the main office.

A man burst out of the final crossway before the entrance and barreled into Samuel, sending him crashing into the wall. Caleb pivoted to knife him when a rotund, heavyset man with unkempt blond hair and flabby limbs rushed out of a door ahead.

Eli Baca.

"Hey!" Samuel growled as he struggled to get control of the attacker's flailing hand and weapon.

"I see him!" Caleb raised his Daemon and fired as Eli bolted for the front door. A shimmer rippled over the man's clothing, an indication he too wore a shield.

But Eli was slow and Caleb was fast, and he closed the distance with ease. He was two meters away—the door ten—when a sharp crack echoed in his head and everything went black.

R

Mia crept down the darkened street toward Eli's chimeral facility. The air felt eerily silent, the splatter of raindrops on the sidewalk the only sound penetrating the gloom—

—she leapt in surprise at the roar of an engine as a shuttle took off from a nearby rooftop.

Well, it was quiet except for that.

She chastised herself for being so skittish and tugged the hood of her new coat lower to peek out from beneath it guardedly.

The entrance to the building was on the next block and across the intersection. Some part of her had expected to find the street in front of it transformed into a river of blood, but there was nothing. Perhaps the rain was washing it away.

She moved as close as she dared to the facility and studied it, perplexed. Everything appeared normal. Two guards stood at relaxed attention outside the doors. No gunfire interrupted the quiet.

What if the assault didn't happen tonight at all? She'd had no reason to assume it would be tonight, none but her desire for it to be so. Or maybe something had gone wrong like she'd feared—

—the doors opened, freeing a cacophony of chaotic noises and startling the guards. Eli burst forth out of the doors at a full run while yelling at his men and gesturing behind him. They dashed inside.

He looked ridiculous, splashing clumsily through the puddles on the sidewalk as he lumbered forward, wheezing from the exertion.

But no one was chasing him.

He was going to get away.

The hilt of the blade she'd purchased sat clenched in a death grip in her hand; she'd been holding it so tightly her fingers had started to cramp.

The edges of her vision blurred. Her awareness narrowed to encompass Eli Baca and nothing else. Drug trafficker, mob minion, violent and brutish thug. A 24th century feudal lord wielding the power of life and death over all he commanded.

An unexpected calmness settled within her as she crossed the street, her pace deliberate but unhurried.

Mia stepped onto the sidewalk in front of him. He failed to recognize her in the long coat and hood, and made to veer around her.

She took a single step sideways to block his path, activated the blade and plunged it into his heart.

Eli was fat, but her blade was far from tiny. A bloom of red unfurled to dye his sweaty shirt crimson as he gaped at her in shock and confusion.

She reached up with her free hand, pulled the hood off and leveled a cold, malevolent glare at him. "You don't own me anymore."

Then she retracted the blade and stepped away. He collapsed at her feet.

The world rushed back in around her. Her heartbeat pounded in her ears and flushed her skin hot. Commotion overflowed the entrance to the facility.

She looked up to see her intelligence agent friend run out the door, gun raised. On spotting her he raced over. His gaze never shifted from her to the body on the ground, not even when he stepped around it to place a hand on her shoulder. "Are you hurt?"

He was bleeding from a cut above his hairline; the blood joined with raindrops to stream down his temple and trail raggedly along his cheek. Separate, different blood seeped from his lower lip.

She swallowed, wondering how her throat could be so dry amidst all this rain. "You are."

He exhaled in a kind of winded scoff. "I'm good. Got whacked in the head is all."

"Caleb!"

The shout drew his attention. He turned toward its source, a stranger exiting the building. "Over here."

When he turned back to her, she cocked an eyebrow. "'Caleb'?"

He shrugged. "Sorry."

The other man jogged up to them, though he limped noticeably and cradled his left arm against his abdomen. He was older, with shoulder-length hair and a slightly wild beard. "Ma'am." He nodded curtly in her direction, then focused on Caleb. "I think everybody's down, but we should blow it soon."

Caleb offered her a hand. "We need to get to a safe distance."

She accepted it and let him lead her across the street while her mind whirled with conflicting thoughts and unfamiliar but heady emotions. She wasn't in shock, but she could be accused of being somewhat dazed.

They continued on to the end of the block before stopping. Caleb produced a small transmitter from his pack and held it out to her. "You're supposed to be on your way to Romane—but seeing as you're here instead, would you like to do the honors?"

She stared at the transmitter, then at the building, then at the transmitter.

"It's okay, you don't have to. I only thought…."

She snatched the transmitter from his grasp. "Damn straight I would."

"Now, you want to—"

"I know how it works."

Eyes fixated on the building, she moved her thumb to the signal trigger and depressed it.

A cascade of explosions ripped apart the walls and night became day as roiling red-gold flames surged upward and outward. The sound followed, a multi-tonal roar that grew as secondary blasts flared. Debris fell to the street alongside the rain, and a dust cloud made its way to them.

Laughter bubbled up from deep in her chest. Not at the people dead inside, for some small part of her heart mourned them. Some of them. No, the laughter was for herself.

She was free.

Caleb gently removed the transmitter from her hand and returned it to his pack. "Congratulations. Vengeance is yours."

She shook her head. "Not vengeance—justice. Punishment meted out for crimes committed."

"Are you going to be okay? We have a bit more work to do here, but after we're done I can help you get clear."

She smiled and started backing down the street. Toward the spaceport. Further, to where there would be stars ahead of her.

"Thank you. But I'm going to be just fine."

∴

Caleb watched her walk away. His brow furrowed, which sent a fresh trickle of blood flowing out of the cut on his head. He'd gotten it when one of Eli's men had hit him with a pole. A damn metal *pole*.

He glanced at the inferno now engulfing the block, then back at Mia, who now rapidly disappeared into the night.

"Don't you dare go after her."

"I didn't say I was."

"But you were thinking it, and I'm telling you, don't."

He huffed a tired breath and crossed his arms against his stomach. "You think you know everything there is to know, so enlighten me—why not?"

Samuel leaned on the façade behind him to take the weight off his injured leg. "You have got to get over this romantic bullshit. We can't afford hearts and flowers in this job." He pointed to the burning building as sirens heralded the approach of emergency personnel. "*This* is your job—this is your life. Blood and death and pain and vengeance and justice. And sometimes it sucks, but it's worth it."

Caleb sighed, but not in resignation. "I know this is the job, and it is worth it. But I refuse to believe it's my life. Not only and not forever."

Samuel pinched the bridge of his nose and waved dismissively with his other hand. "Fucking romantic."

Caleb turned back to gaze down the street...and found it empty. She was gone. He felt a faint tinge of regret, but he put it aside. Something told him she was, in fact, going to be just fine.

AFTERWORD TO *SOLATIUM*
INCLUDED IN *CRIME & PUNISHMENT*

In one of my books, a character muses that "morality could not be spawned by tweaking a few genes or shutting off a few neurons. So though humanity conquered the very stars, it remained unable to conquer the darkness within."

I visit this notion often in my writing—the idea that all the advances in technology, medical marvels and scientific discoveries we could hope for will not change the nature of the human soul. What if we pursue genetic enhancements, cybernetics, long lifespans, even colonization of other planets, only to find that we're still simply human, with all the same faults, weaknesses, foibles—and strengths—that we've always had? Can we ever grow beyond our fundamental nature, flaws and all?

The character quoted above goes on to observe that even in the 24th century, when humanity had spread to the stars and settled over 100 worlds, the weak continued to be preyed upon by the strong in the prolific shadows not policed by any government.

Solatium shines a light into the crevices of one of those shadows. It's a story about criminals and those who punish them, but mostly it's a story about the struggle to keep hold of one's soul in the face of so much darkness. It features two characters who go on to play prominent roles in my *Aurora Rising* trilogy, set twelve years later. Mia's backstory is hinted at in *Starshine* (*Aurora Rising Book One*), but it begged to be told in full, and I could imagine no better venue for it than this anthology.

APOGEE

APOGEE

AN AURORA RHAPSODY

AR

SHORT STORY

G. S. JENNSEN

"Its leaders believe the Alliance is powerful enough to be both—a democracy on election days and a dictatorship on every other day—but they're wrong. No government should be so powerful.

"It's time someone demonstrates the error in their thinking."

The Earth Alliance rules 82 worlds, controlling an empire that spans a third of the Milky Way. But when its leaders stray too far from the democratic principles on which it was founded, one colony—one group of daring rebels—will risk everything in order to reclaim their freedom.

Set a quarter century before *STARSHINE: Aurora Rising Book One (Amaranthe #1)*, *APOGEE* tells the story of the fateful decisions and critical opening moves of the First Crux War between the Earth Alliance and the Senecan Federation, the repercussions of which will ripple forward across decades and shape the world of *Aurora Rhapsody* forever.

*

Apogee is a bit unusual in that none of the major characters from the Aurora Rhapsody *novels appear in it. The repercussions of its events, however, have a tremendous impact on the plot and the characters of the series. While the story takes place over two decades before* Starshine, *the first novel, within the context of the overall plot* Apogee *is best read between* Sidespace *and* Dissonance, *though it stands on its own as well.*

DRAMATIS PERSONAE

Stefan Marano
Special Operations intelligence agent,
Senecan Federation Division of Intelligence.
Faction: *Senecan Federation*

Commander Helena Lekkas
Pilot, EA NE Regional Command.
Faction: *Senecan Federation*

Brigadier Eleni Gianno
XO, Earth Alliance Military Seneca Headquarters.
Faction: *Senecan Federation*

Darien Terzi
Director,
Earth Alliance Division of Intelligence, Seneca Division.
Faction: *Senecan Federation*

Aristide Vranas
Former Mayor of Cavare, capital city of Seneca.
Faction: *Senecan Federation*

"The end is in the beginning and lies far ahead."

— *Ralph Ellison*

2297

(25 YEARS BEFORE THE EVENTS OF STARSHINE)

SENECA

EARTH ALLIANCE COLONY
CAVARE, CAPITAL CITY

Moonlight cast the man's wife's skin in ghostly silver as he placed a soft kiss on her forehead. He hadn't meant to wake her, but she stirred before he could slip away, blinking to reveal bleary, unfocused irises.

"It's okay, Frannie, don't get up. I'll be home in a few days."

She nodded sleepily, mumbled, "Love you...good luck at the symposium," and rolled over. When her breathing evened out in slumber once more, he tiptoed out of the bedroom and down the hall to crack the door to his daughter's room. A mess of curls poked out of the bedcovers to fan out on the pillow. He smiled to himself and eased the door shut.

He didn't attempt to sneak a peek into his son's room. The boy had developed preternatural senses and would be wide awake in an instant. In truth he'd probably awoken the instant there was a sound in the hallway...but if so, he didn't emerge to inquire as to the reason for his father's early departure.

It was for the best. At fourteen, his son was not only no longer a child but also disconcertingly clever, and he would likely pose too-astute questions the man didn't dare answer.

Once outside he tossed his bag onto the passenger seat of his skycar. The first steel-hued rays of dawn breached the mountains in the distance as he lifted off.

Twenty minutes later he stepped up to the security checkpoint entry for the Alliance outpost military base on the periphery of Cavare and waved his palm at the identity check. The officer on duty examined the readout briefly. "You're cleared for entry, sir, but may I ask what your purpose here is today?"

He canted his head at the young man. "Check your screen again, Lieutenant."

The lieutenant's brow furrowed, but he instinctively obeyed the implied order. "Uh, right. Sir. You're cleared for…whatever your reason is for being here." Squared shoulders preceded a crisp forward hand motion.

It wasn't unusual behavior for the man, as an Intelligence agent, to visit the Earth Alliance's largest military base on Seneca, and he'd done so multiple times for legitimate reasons. And as an Intelligence agent he wasn't required to disclose the purpose of his visit to anyone who challenged him.

He gestured a thanks and walked through the checkpoint, a wry smirk hovering on his lips.

My purpose is to start a war. Have a nice day.

ᴙ

LUNAR SSR CENTER

Seneca Stellar System

He didn't gape at any of the other passengers on the military shuttle. Tension radiated off the soldiers to vibrate in the air so thickly he now inhaled it with every breath; he didn't have to inspect them to realize they were on edge and prepping for a fight.

Personally, he hoped the fight wouldn't commence until he was airborne again. He wasn't a soldier—though he could impersonate one if need be—and this day was going to be difficult enough without wading through close-quarters combat.

His visit to the military base had been a brief one. On his arrival he was quickly directed through several dark service hallways to a small landing pad and ushered onto the shuttle. He assumed this meant his traveling companions were also members of the resistance, but no one had so much as spoken a greeting during the forty-minute trip.

The Lunar Special Support and Research Center sprawled across a region of the moon that had been largely spared the brutality of relentless asteroid bombardment over the millennia, at least compared to the rest of the satellite. The test fields of the research facility stretched for hundreds of kilometers beyond the Center itself, and the crimson beacons denoting their various boundaries flickered against the otherwise ashen surface.

The shuttle dropped through the first of multiple force fields. The outer barrier protected the Center from meteoroids and other minor space objects that would burn up harmlessly if the moon had a natural atmosphere. Next came the triple-layer fields keeping the artificially generated atmosphere inside. The layers were a redundant safety measure, as a failure of the system would be catastrophic to the facility's equipment but more so to the people working there.

Even the multiple redundancies did little to assuage his disquiet, and he allowed the soldiers to disembark before exiting the shuttle. If it weren't for the paved surface beneath his feet and the structures visible at the opposite end of the platform, he would have sworn he was treading into open space and without so much as an environment suit to protect him. From here the discreet shimmer of the force fields provided only the slightest blur to the blackness of space and its expanse of stars.

He liked to believe he could handle virtually any situation he encountered, no matter how dire. But everyone had a weakness, and he'd never managed to get comfortable with open space...maybe because he couldn't control it.

On taking a step away from the shuttle, he was promptly overwhelmed by the expected but still unpleasant sense he was about to float off into the void. A wave of dizziness threatened to take hold, and he searched around for a signpost, anxious to get inside some-thing, *anything*.

He grabbed a passing officer by the arm. The man jerked away and leveled an intimidating glower at him.

"Excuse me, I'm sorry. I need directions to Lab EE12c."

The officer scowled at him for a beat then jerked his head. "See the last building on the left? The building behind it."

"Thank you." He hurried off in the direction indicated, toward the illusory but nevertheless seductive shelter.

ᴙ

The notion that one of its colonies would go to war with the mighty Earth Alliance, eighty-two worlds and fourteen billion peo-ple strong, was as ludicrous as the proposition that man would discover a means to circumvent special relativity and develop star-ship drives capable of velocities far exceeding the speed of light.

No one had believed the latter possible until it was achieved. So, too, would it be with the former.

"This is what we're counting on. The Alliance hasn't faced a successful colonial rebellion in a hundred fifty years of extra-solar expansion. It no longer believes such a thing can be accomplished, but we'll turn the Alliance's hubris against it. The slow response of its goliath bureaucratic machinery will give us time—time to get more ships out of production and into space as well as time to sub-due any lingering resistance and gain full control of the government and military on Seneca."

Darien Terzi sounded as if he were trying to convince himself of the validity of the plan more than those present, Brigadier Eleni Gianno mused. She hoped the strength of his conviction did not fail him when the blood started flowing.

She clasped her hands at the small of her back, adopting a com-fortable yet formal posture. "The military will not be as difficult to secure as one would expect. Eighty-three percent of the enlisted and seventy-one percent of the officers Commodore rank and be-low are Senecan-born. If presented with a persuasive argument for independence and an assertive demonstration of leadership, they will fall in line."

Terzi nodded in acceptance. "And the higher ranking officers? The ones rotating through on a tour of duty?"

"They will not be so amenable. But we know who they are. Given the recent unrest, there's never been a wider rift between our people and theirs. When we make our move, they will be detained and held in a secure location until we can put them on an Earth-bound vessel and send them on their way."

A laugh bubbled up from somewhere behind her left shoulder. "Your plan may work for most of the officers, assuming you've got enough muscle on your side, but General Castillo is a first-class prick brandishing an ego far larger than the impressively sized gun he carries. I doubt he will agree to go quietly."

She regarded the source of the comment with mild curiosity. Aristide Vranas was the ex-Mayor of Seneca's capital city, Cavare. He had been deposed when the Alliance sent in its lackeys to take over key government postings three months ago in the aftermath of the worker riots. If asked to consider the question, she would conclude she liked the man. He possessed an unpretentious, easy charisma and a dry sense of humor that never got in the way of a fundamentally earnest nature.

"I doubt he will agree to go at all, which is why I will be forced to disable him and may be forced to kill him. But either way, that's on me."

He gave her a small smile in lieu of a reply before returning his gaze to the window.

They were gathered in a small conference room in a remote corner of the Lunar SSR Center. This close to the precipice, meeting groundside held too many risks—too many Alliance loyalists skulking the halls of power.

Terzi had taken up pacing the length of the room. As the director of the Senecan field office of the Earth Alliance Ministry of Intelligence, he had as much to lose as she did. The sole difference between her fate and his if this venture failed would be the locations of their confinement until their executions.

On his next pivot he directed his attention to Vranas. "Aristide, when we're done here I want you to get back to Cavare then stay out of sight until it's time to go public. Local Alliance officials will suspect your involvement, and we can't risk them grabbing you. I assume the speech is ready?"

"The speech has been ready for years, waiting on the proper moment for its delivery to arrive. Let me worry about the public. You worry about the logistics."

If Terzi took offense at the barb, he didn't show it. "I have agents tailing the provisional mayor and governor. When I give the word, both will be taken into custody. We'll keep them isolated until I can get them on Gianno's ship to Earth. Fucking interlopers."

He dragged a hand down his face. "Once we declare we are cutting ties with the Earth Alliance, coordination and proper timing are crucial. A number of things must happen in the first hour or we will lose control of the situation. But the pieces are in place, and we're as ready as we're going to be." He looked to them for confirmation and received it.

Vranas asked the most obvious and consequential question. "When?"

Gianno responded. "The Alliance First Brigade from Arcadia will reach its closest point to Seneca in three hours. We *want* it to be close—that timing you mentioned. If we miss this window, we won't see a better one for six weeks so...." She lifted her chin. "I advise we go now."

"Agreed. Give me a minute to arrange a few matters."

Eleni moved to the window beside Vranas. A sea of stars gave way to Seneca's familiar profile as the moon continued onward in its perpetual rotation.

"Have you ever been to Earth, Brigadier?"

"No, I haven't. I did my off-world training on Arcadia and Messium."

"I attended a convention there four years ago. Lovely place. Enormous sapphire-blue oceans everywhere you look."

"I'll have to take your word for it, as I suspect the only way I'll ever step foot on Earth at this point is for a military tribunal, and I don't intend to allow that to happen."

Terzi reappeared next to her, and she abandoned the view to focus on him. The hour was late, and the time for talk to give way to action was upon them. "Has your agent arrived? I need to brief him and go over the ship's capabilities, but we're now on an exceptionally tight schedule."

"He's waiting outside. I'll ask him to come in."

The man who walked in bore a closer resemblance to a banker or a corporate executive than an Intelligence agent. Neatly styled, wavy black hair complemented a distinguished jawline and iced-cobalt irises. He carried himself with quiet, resolute confidence as he approached her and extended a hand. "Ma'am."

They continued sizing one another up with practiced eyes as they shook hands. "A pleasure to meet you, Agent…?"

"Marano. Stefan Marano."

ℛ

Director Terzi and Brigadier Gianno departed after showing Stefan to the hangar bay, and he took the opportunity of a few minutes alone to study the reconnaissance craft. The muted bronze hull appeared to draw in the light surrounding it, giving it a faint lustrous sheen. Sleekly aerodynamic, the frame's edges cut sharply enough he made a note to give them a wide berth.

He did reach out to run his fingertips along the body, however, enjoying the smooth coolness of the material. Senecan designed and constructed, it was not merely more elegant than anything the Alliance produced, it was *better* than anything the Alliance produced. Faster. Stealthier—

The air shifted around him, heralding a new guest. A woman joined him beside the ship; he continued his inspection of the hull while inspecting her in his peripheral vision. Dressed in standard-issue Earth Alliance BDUs, she was nearly as tall as him and muscular in the way most young military officers were, with shoulder-length dark hair bound back in a tight tail.

He acknowledged her with a casual nod. "I admittedly don't know ships, but this is a hell of a good-looking one."

"First of her kind, and I get to fly her." She stuck out a hand. "Commander Helena Lekkas. I'll be your pilot for the operation. Also the weapons officer, navigator and mechanic. You know, now that I think about it, why is it you're coming along?"

Ah, so she was a smartass. It seemed to be a hazard of the piloting profession. He was fine with banter, but not until he controlled the relationship dynamic.

"Because this is a top-secret Intelligence black operation outside the purview of the military. And you're not the weapons officer—I am. Any more answers will have to wait until we've departed."

"That so? I assure you, I can hit a target perfectly well."

"Not with this weapon."

She glared at him silently for several seconds. "If you say so. Let me finish the preflight check, and we'll be on our way."

ℛ

STEALTH RECONNAISSANCE VESSEL

Seneca Lunar Orbit

"In the wake of the declaration by ousted government officials that Seneca was formally severing ties with the Earth Alliance, martial law is now in effect across the colony."

The news feed cut to vids of armored combat vehicles patrolling the streets and soldiers in riot gear arresting protesters outside one of the government buildings in downtown Cavare.

"We're receiving scattered reports of weapons fire on the grounds of the Alliance military base. We're unable to confirm these accounts, as our reporters are being denied entry to the base and a barrier is preventing

aerial coverage. We do have footage coming in of a skirmish between law-enforcement officers and military personnel near the Civil Administration Building.

"It is clear the conditions on the streets tonight are very fluid, and we urge everyone to stay indoors if possible. What isn't clear is exactly who, if anyone, is in control of Seneca."

They drifted 0.1 megameters above the lunar surface, having departed the Lunar SSR Center before violence erupted. Several hours remained until their mission began, so for now they could do nothing but watch the news feeds and, knowing something of what was in fact transpiring, wonder impotently whether the outcome would be in their favor.

The police and security departments had in reality never been under Alliance control and would not have assisted in enforcing martial law even if there were not a coup underway. Events inside the military base were certain to be far dicier.

The mission parameters forbade any contact with other resistance members, or anyone for that matter, given the small but non-zero chance someone in the Alliance could be eavesdropping. So they waited.

By the time the media figured out what was happening, it was already over, at least on the ground. The press conferences and prepared statements began to roll in fast and furious, all urging calm and all speaking the language of a new, independent, democratic government.

As expected, the Alliance ordered the Arcadia First Brigade to Seneca to establish a blockade. The news feed reporter wore a grave expression as he explained how commercial craft trying to leave Seneca would be ordered to land or risk being shot down.

Also as expected, Alliance forces on the nearby worlds of Elathan and Krysk, the only colonies in range possessing a combat-ready military presence, were put on full alert and two regiments ordered to Seneca to assist with the blockade. The meager details the media possessed scrolled in a repetitive loop on the feed overlay, and he soon tuned them out.

"Why did you decide to become a revolutionary?"

Stefan kept his gaze on the silhouettes of the planet and its satellite beneath them. "My kids. The Alliance claims to be a democracy, but it threw the principle out the window the second we caused it a tiny bit of discomfort. Overtaxing us because we thrive—then using the money to prop up its bloated bureaucracy—isn't good policy, but marching in and removing our elected leaders by fiat due to a few worker riots? 'Disappearing' people who speak out against it? That's not a democracy, that's a dictatorship.

"Its leaders believe the Alliance is powerful enough to be both—a democracy on election days and a dictatorship on every other day—but they're wrong. No government should be so powerful. It's time someone demonstrates the error in their thinking."

"Hmm." Lekkas drummed her fingers on the dash. Having completed a thorough exploration of the new ship an hour ago, she had little to do until the action started. "What's all that have to do with your kids?"

"I don't want them to grow up in a dictatorship, obviously, or under any regime that can act as it chooses without repercussions. They have bright futures ahead of them, and I want better for their lives."

She didn't inquire further. She wasn't exactly the talkative sort, but in this instance he chose to prod her. "What about you? Why are you here?"

"Live free or die, man. That's my motto."

He laughed. "Is it really?"

"Nah. Gianno was a persuasive woman, particularly after my Alliance superiors grounded me for smarting off about what were unequivocally stupid orders."

He'd read her file and agreed they had been stupid orders. "Do you have any kids?" He also knew the answer to this question, but better for her to tell him.

"Daughter. She's four. Wants to follow in her mom's footsteps and fly starships. I'm not convinced I'm going to be able to stop her, stubborn brat."

"Children do turn out to have wills and minds of their own. Husband?"

She snorted. "Hell, no. Her father—" She snapped up straight in the cockpit chair as the primary scanner lit up in red blips. "Looks like the Alliance brigade is here. Took it long enough."

He blew out a long, weighty breath, paralyzed by the weight of the actions ahead of him but unwilling to display weakness in front of his companion.

He hadn't wanted this mission. Terzi had thrown praise and platitudes in his direction, called him an honest man and a true believer and someone the resistance could depend on. Perhaps most of it was accurate, perhaps not. He *was* a patriot—to Seneca, not the Alliance—and he understood the necessity of this war. Its time had come, and he felt compelled to play his part. But he selfishly preferred someone else bear the guilt guaranteed to arrive once the adrenaline relinquished its grasp.

Suspicious it had grown wild, he ran a hand through his normally tame hair. "All right, we need to sneak in behind them. Do it now, while they're distracted getting themselves situated. Remember, staying undetected takes top priority. If they spot us, we're dead and this is all for naught."

"Not to worry. This ship has a custom cloaking shield built using original tech. The Alliance has never seen its kind. They don't know what to hunt for and wouldn't recognize it if they did detect it."

"I appreciate that. Still, don't take any chances."

She grumbled as they accelerated away from the moon. "Pretty sure I don't take orders from you."

The last thing he needed was a renegade pilot. He circled around her chair until he was between her and the dash. "And I'm pretty sure so long as I'm on this ship, you *do*. Intelligence mission, not military, remember?"

She stared at him, rich emerald eyes piercing through him. Then her chin dipped a fraction and she returned her focus to the HUD. "Whatever you say, *Agent.*" Her fingertips glided along the virtual controls. "Speaking of which, I didn't get a name."

"No, you didn't."

ᴚ

A growing crowd of vessels orbited the planet—a hodgepodge of long, bulky commercial carriers; lightweight merchant runners; and elaborate, tricked-out civilian transports.

They were blocked by a brigade-strength collection of Alliance warships. For now the warships kept their distance, maintaining a 0.5 megameter stretch of space between the departing craft and the unofficial front line of the blockade.

A handful had tried to make a run for it and been intercepted by fighters. Thus far the civilian vessels had always retreated, and shots had yet to be fired.

A number of the civilian vessels were equipped with laser weapons—certainly more than the Alliance contingent had anticipated. Many of them were effectively ringers, high-powered corporate craft sporting almost as much weaponry and hull shielding as military ships.

Stefan checked the time as unease gnawed at his gut. The civilians ostensibly wanting to leave were here, the Alliance warships were here...but the expected resistance ships were late. Had Gianno encountered greater difficulties on the ground than anticipated? Had she failed altogether? He had no way to know and didn't dare risk a comm to find out.

They floated silently and fully cloaked in the middle of the Alliance blockade, trying to imitate a hole in space. Lekkas was peering out the viewport, scrutinizing the hulls of several vessels that lurked worryingly close.

"Think they'll hear me if I start singing the Greek national anthem?"

"What?"

She rolled her eyes. "Nothing. When's the cavalry scheduled to show?"

"Twenty minutes ago."

She arched a brow and settled back into her chair.

He tried for small talk to divert their attention from the ticking clock. "Have you ever seen live combat?"

"A year or so ago, when the Triene cartel made a hard run to claim Bellici for its own. It took us a week to decimate them and another week to run off what was left. Couple of smaller skirmishes before then."

"Why did—" He cut off as the imposing contours of two military cruisers accelerated in from starboard to take up positions between the civilian vessels and the Alliance formation. "Can we listen in on the wideband communications without alerting them to our presence?"

"Yep." She punched in a series of instructions, and a new screen joined the already crowded HUD to display the transmission details. A few seconds later the audio feed kicked in, and an unfamiliar voice reverberated in the cabin.

Admiral Himura (EAS *Fuzhou*): *"Captains of the EAS* Inchon *and* EAS Verdun, *you are in contravention of direct orders from Earth Alliance Strategic Command. If you do not surrender control of your vessels and retreat immediately, you will be deemed mutineers and subject to general courts-martial."*

There was no delay in the response.

Unidentified (SFS *Verdun*): *"That's a negative. We have commandeered all Alliance vessels on Senecan soil in the name of the Senecan Federation."*

Admiral Himura (EAS *Fuzhou*): *What 'Federation?' You have no allies. You have nowhere to run. You are ordered to stand down now."*

Stefan's hands tightened on the cockpit chair's backrest as half a dozen frigates cleared the atmosphere below and joined the rebel cruisers. Maybe his involvement wouldn't be required. He found himself hoping the Alliance would open fire and absolve him of responsibility.

The luminous halo of Seneca's sun above the arc of the planet dimmed as two additional groupings of Alliance warships advanced. He realized his foot was tapping loudly on the skid-resistant flooring and forced it still. "This should be the regiments from Elathan and Krysk."

Lekkas glanced over her shoulder at him. "They're on our side, right?"

"That was the plan. Can't say if the plan succeeded."

Admiral Himura (EAS Fuzhou): "Fourth and Seventh Regiments, adopt positions flanking the mutinying ships."

Unidentified (SFS Ankara): "We must refuse to follow that order. In accordance with the directives of the Elathan and Krysk governing bodies issued as of 1021.0930 Galactic, the military commands stationed on those worlds pledge their allegiance to the newly formed Senecan Federation."

They both sighed in relief. If the rebels on Elathan and Krysk hadn't been able to gain control of the dispatched vessels, this would've become a rather lopsided battle and a damn short war.

The silence had begun to grow uncomfortably long when the reply came.

Admiral Himura (EAS Fuzhou): "Very well. This 'Senecan Federation' and its members are seditionists in violation of the Second Earth Alliance Constitution of 2146. Any and all actions it undertakes are illegal, null, and void.

"Any Earth Alliance military personnel who, whether through affirmative acts or by inaction, assist these seditionists are guilty of treason and will be held accountable. To all present military personnel: you have five minutes to respond accordingly."

Lekkas chuckled. "Bet more than one scuffle just broke out on board those ships."

"Any second thoughts?"

Her head shook tersely. "We're all traitors now."

"It's not traitorous to want to be free."

"Oh, God, you're an idealist."

He opened his mouth to argue, then stopped. Idealism wasn't an easy outlook to maintain in his profession, but it kept him sane. "I suppose I am. It's served me well enough so far."

She opted not to challenge him on it, instead checking all the HUD screens for the Nth time. "We wait for Gianno, correct?"

"Correct."

She nodded slowly, and together they stared out the viewport. It felt as if the fabric of spacetime itself had frozen, the universe holding its breath together with them as the decreed deadline drew ever closer. Every object in the galaxy was surely fixated on this point, eager to witness what transpired on the other side of the event horizon.

Thirty seconds of the five minutes remained when a new arrival emerged out of the glare of the sun, rising from beneath the demarcation line to take up a position in the center of the rebel contingent.

Like the craft he currently occupied, its hull was a muted bronze, though the sun's reflected light painted it burnished copper. Also like the reconnaissance craft, it sported sleek curves and knifed edges.

It was, of course, far larger than the recon craft—around fifteen hundred percent larger in fact, and twice as large as the Alliance cruisers. It wasn't a dreadnought, as hiding the construction of one of those behemoths would've been a doomed undertaking, but it was the next closest thing. Built from the ground up using Senecan materials, technology and weaponry, it was the flagship of what would hopefully become a significant fleet of Senecan Federation warships.

But that all depended on the outcome of this confrontation, here, today. Arguably it depended on the outcome of future confrontations as well, but those would never occur in the absence of a victory here.

Unidentified: *"This is the* SFS Thermopylae. *On behalf of the Senecan Federation, I request all Earth Alliance vessels desist in their blockade of civilian traffic to and from Senecan space. Further, I request such vessels depart the Senecan Stellar System forthwith, as they are trespassing on Senecan Federation territory."*

Admiral Himura *(EAS Fuzhou): "There is no such thing as Senecan Federation 'territory.' You are all deserters and turncoats, and you will be treated as such. You need to be very, very careful what you do next, or you will find yourself with a war on your hands."* The Admiral's voice bled barely controlled incredulity and rage.

Unidentified (SFS Thermopylae): *"We do not desire a war. As stated in the declaration transmitted to Prime Minister Ioannou, the leadership of the Earth Alliance Assembly and EASC Board Chairman Breveski, we intend to institute our own government, one based on legitimate self-determination and the principles of freedom the Alliance once adhered to but has now abandoned.*

"We expect the Earth Alliance government to allow any colonies that wish to join the Senecan Federation to withdraw from the Alliance without incident. Our desire is to coexist peacefully alongside the Alliance, but we will not be subject to its rule any longer."

Stefan's hands trembled on the backrest; annoyed, he clasped one over the other in an attempt to subdue them. "Move into position."

Her hands swept across the controls. "And by 'position' you mean approximately ten centimeters beneath the laser turrets of this Alliance cruiser here?"

"I do."

"Got it. Piece of cake." The reply was delivered through gritted teeth and a clenched jaw as they oh-so-carefully skimmed forward and rose toward the hulking shadow. Though they flew in a deliberate, cautious manner, the cruiser's hull raced by overhead. It was a long vessel at three hundred and ten meters, and the weapons were located a third of the way down the underside.

"Careful—don't crash into the hull!"

"I'm...not...." A distinct growl had joined the gritted teeth and clenched jaw.

The large weapon housing hung beneath the frame ahead of them. They slowed to a stop less than ten meters behind it.

"Hope they don't decide to move before we're done."

Stefan's voice came out clipped as he leaned into the HUD beside her. Would a second chair in the cockpit have been too much to ask? "Hold us steady. I'm locking onto the target."

The HUD screen directly in front of him became a reticle. It pulsed as he painstakingly maneuvered it until the center settled on the subtly gleaming bow of the *SFS Thermopylae*.

"What's so special about this weapon?"

"We stole the Alliance schem flow and amped up the power so it mimics a cruiser's weaponry. The targeting system works a bit differently as a result."

Admiral Himura (EAS Fuzhou): "I will say again: stand down now, relinquish all Alliance ships and materials in your possession and present yourself for court-martial proceedings."

Unidentified (SFS Thermopylae): "Negative."

Stefan exhaled. Point of no return, come and gone. "Firing."

The laser streaked out from beneath the viewport. The shot was larger and more powerful than those generated by the weaponry typically found on a recon craft. It also utilized the ytterbium-crystal pulse laser materials wielded by Alliance military weapons, so anyone looking in their direction would swear the fire had originated from the Alliance cruiser situated directly above Stefan and Lekkas.

The *Thermopylae* was in motion, denying the sieging warships a convenient target for the attack it had been likely to provoke. As it streaked across the line of blockaded ships, a large commercial transport emerged from beneath it headed in the opposite direction.

The laser struck the civilian vessel full-on broadside.

Lacking sufficient shielding, it ruptured into a ball of roiling white and coral as both the active impulse engine and the thankfully dormant sLume superluminal drive exploded.

The *Thermopylae* returned fire. Everyone returned fire, and space lit up in an infernal clamor of interweaving lasers and detonations. The cruiser above them accelerated to port, and bedlam unfurled in its wake.

Lekkas had fallen back in her chair, leaving their ship drifting and exposed. "You...you hit a *civilian* ship! How did you miss a bloody battlecruiser?"

Shock replaced horror as the dominant expression animating her face when she discovered Stefan's gun pointed at her chest.

"Your psych profile indicates you respond to extreme stress with enhanced reaction speeds and sharper focus. So get us out of here in one piece, would you?"

Her mouth snapped into a thin, hard line as her pupils contracted. "Yes, *sir*."

She seized the controls once more, and he re-holstered his gun. The floor pitched beneath his feet as they too accelerated, albeit away from the cruiser, and banked hard. He stumbled away from the dash and grabbed the top of her chair to prevent being thrown to the floor.

A fighter shot past their bow as they dove away, and in the next blink they were dodging two additional fighters and skimming the hull of a frigate. His stomach lurched, and if it hadn't been many hours since he'd eaten, he would've vomited its contents.

The viewport briefly cleared—then another frigate was bearing down on their location. It didn't know they were there, but it was moving far too fast to divert in any event.

"Shit!" Lekkas yanked the ship vertical, sending him thudding to the floor and skidding into the main cabin. His head slammed into the leg of a workstation as they finally leveled off.

"Okay back there?"

He massaged the back of his head and struggled to his feet. "That wasn't funny."

"You should've strapped in to the jump seat."

"Given your certification scores, I expected it to be a smoother ride."

"Must have been the extreme stress affecting my skills."

When he reached the cockpit, he was relieved to see the surrounding space beginning to thin in a more permanent fashion. They had soared above the bulk of the fighting and were now racing away. Their job here was done, and the campaign would be won or lost without their participation.

"Are you going to point a gun at me again?"

"No. I simply needed to short-circuit your tirade and refocus you on the task at hand."

She swung her chair around and crossed her arms tightly over her chest. "Asshole. How could you miss? Do you know how many innocent civilians you killed?"

"Seventeen."

"Are you kidding? That transport could hold four hundred people. Even if it wasn't full to capacity—"

"There were seventeen people on the ship. A skeleton crew. And I didn't miss. It was my target."

She stared at him in disbelief. "*Why?*"

He thought about Frannie, believing her husband was off at an engineering symposium planning a spaceport expansion and new levtram routes. He'd scheduled a series of messages to her to be delivered once the coup began so she didn't worry. What would she think of him if she knew what he had just done, what he *did* for a living?

He met Lekkas' furious stare with an equally cool one. "Because that was my mission."

"Your mission? No. Your mission was to simulate an attack by the Alliance cruiser on our new warship, instigating the *Thermopylae* to open fire."

"No, that was *your* mission. My mission was to hit the civilian vessel. It was specifically chosen since it would be all but empty, thus minimizing casualties, and Brigadier Gianno made certain the *Thermopylae* crossed its path at the pivotal moment.

"See, nobody will care how many people actually died. They'll only care that the Alliance opened fire on a defenseless merchant vessel. Public opinion will be on our side, which means more colonies will offer support or even join the Federation. Money will flow to our cause so we can pay for the ships that are essential if we expect to prevail."

Outside the viewport an amber burst flared. The sun was now behind them, and the eruption created a stark contrast to the space beyond it. Another ship destroyed, on and by one side or the other.

She shook her head as if to tangibly deny his point. "So that's the real reason I wasn't trusted to handle the shooting—and rightfully so. It wasn't required. A shot at the *Thermopylae* would have been enough."

"Possibly. Not my call to make, but I can't disagree with the logic. We need every advantage we can create in these early hours and days if we're to stand a snowball's chance in Hell at winning this war. The Alliance military has nearly six thousand warships, and that's before you start counting the fighters and support craft. We need them arguing over how to proceed instead of sending their entire damn fleet to Seneca. We need them doing what they do best: debating, hedging and creating a dozen committees to draw up rules of engagement. We need *time*."

"Why lie to me?"

"I didn't lie. I implied, you inferred."

"Don't play semantics with me. I'm not one of your marks. So…." She tossed her arms weakly in the air. "What now?"

"Now we follow the plan. We go home and go our separate ways. We keep our secret, no matter what happens—kidnapping, torture or a billion-credit bribe be damned, we *keep our secret*. Lastly, you stop having a nervous breakdown. You didn't kill those people. I did. You sleep well at night because their blood isn't on your hands, and I sleep well at night because it was…necessary."

"*Necessary*. I refuse to believe that."

Stefan shrugged. "Believe what you want. I believe their sacrifice will save far more lives in the long run—and that *is* our goal. If it helps, which I doubt it does, their families will be well taken care of. Our leaders will set a precedent by demonstrating the Senecan Federation honors its fallen war heroes."

The burden of having started a war in which tens of thousands and perhaps tens of millions would die was a heavy one, but one he'd been prepared to bear. The burden of starting the war by murdering civilians...well, it wasn't as if he hadn't known it would be heavier.

He wasn't a soldier, and dammit but he didn't want to have been here.

The justifications stumbled over one another in a ragged loop in his mind. Lives would ultimately be saved as a result. War meant the spilling of blood. It meant death, and he'd be blindingly naïve to assert otherwise. But war also brought the prospect of a new world, a better world. He had to believe it was worth it.

Lekkas patched in to the *Thermopylae*'s internal comms so they could monitor the opening salvos of the clash. The chatter provided a welcome distraction from the troubled ruminations of his conscience.

Brigadier Gianno (SFS Thermopylae): *"Elathan Seventh Regiment, your sole mission is to take out the* Fuzhou. *Cut the head off the snake, and do it now. Krysk Fourth Regiment, run interference and occupy the frigates protecting the* Fuzhou."

As they swung around on nearing the Lunar SSR Center, the full expanse of the battle spread out before them. The smaller, all-but-defenseless merchant vessels had vacated the area, leaving the military warships and armed civilian craft free to wreak havoc without fear of collateral damage. Most of the warships were outwardly identical, which made it difficult to judge the ebb and flow of the conflict. But it hardly mattered in an arena littered with debris and illuminated by incessant fire and explosions.

Once, humanity's warriors had killed using swords and spears. Now they did so using weapons whose power approached the fury of a sun.

Brigadier Gianno (SFS *Thermopylae): "Let's show them exactly what this ship can do. Don't hold anything back for the next battle, or there may not be a next battle. I see an Alliance cruiser and frigate lingering too close to one another W 43° –6° Z. Also, they're harassing Auxiliary Group Three. Make them regret it."*

The *Thermopylae* cut through the fog of war, aggressively engaging an Alliance cruiser as it maneuvered with remarkable agility through the chaos. Attacks from multiple fighters and a damaged frigate splashed off its defense shields like rain off a pitched roof.

It was a beautiful ship, quick and powerful. A ship worthy of a new federation.

Stefan hoped the people building that federation proved themselves worthy of it.

AFTERWORD TO *APOGEE*
INCLUDED IN *THE GALAXY CHRONICLES*

Space has fascinated me since I was a small child. When I was old enough to dream such things, I wanted to be the scientist who invented faster-than-light space travel. Alas, that wasn't likely to happen, so instead I decided to write stories in which it had already been accomplished.

We live in a time of rapidly advancing technology. Revolutions in medicine and computer intelligence lurk just around the corner. People increasingly talk about strong AI, transhumanism and the singularity as foreseeable events. Meanwhile, the question of what it will mean to be human in the face of these developments hangs unanswered in the air.

So, what if we colonize the stars? What if we create true AI, and it doesn't go Skynet on us? What if it DOES go Skynet on us, but we reign it in? What if we cure diseases, turn ourselves into cyborgs with synthetic enhancements and live for hundreds of years?

What if we do all these things, only to find that we're still simply human, with all the same faults, weaknesses, foibles—and strengths—that we've always had? Can we ever grow beyond our fundamental nature, flaws and all? Should we, or are we stronger with them?

Underlying the massive space battles, alien invasions and random supernovas, I try to write stories that ask (and perhaps suggest answers to) these questions. Stories filled with characters who fight, struggle, love and betray, fail and triumph—and through it all try to do better, to be better. And a few who don't.

Apogee is, in a technical sense, a prequel to my *Aurora Rising* trilogy, though the events in *Apogee* precede it by a quarter century. When *Aurora Rising* opens, we find a galaxy divided. People live under an uneasy détente among the mammoth Earth Alliance, the defiant Senecan Federation and a handful of wealthy independent colonies. When a powerful force threatens humanity's continued existence, their only chance to survive is to put aside their differences and unite against the threat. But despite the clear need to do so, the sins of the past...complicate matters.

Apogee shines a light on that past, telling the story of the fateful decisions and critical opening moves of a war whose repercussions will ripple forward across decades. The war is a story all its own, worthy of a far more fulsome telling...which is something I very well may do in the future. First, though, there are a few questions raised by *Aurora Rising* that need answering.

RESTLESS II

RESTLESS

VOL. II

AN
AURORA
RISING
SHORT STORY

G. S. JENNSEN

Restless II contains spoilers for the events of the _Aurora Rising_ trilogy (_Starshine, Vertigo, Transcendence_)

This is the only story that comes with a spoiler warning and the strong recommendation to not read it until you've finished the first trilogy, Aurora Rising. Why? Well, that would be a spoiler, too, right?

Restless II _acts as a meaningful bridge between the end of_ Aurora Rising _and the beginning of the first_ Aurora Renegades _novel,_ Sidespace, _so once you've read_ Transcendence _, dive in and enjoy!_

DRAMATIS PERSONAE

Alexis 'Alex' Solovy
Starship pilot, scout and space explorer; Prevo.
Daughter of Miriam and David Solovy.
Faction: *Earth Alliance*

Caleb Marano
Former Special Operations intelligence agent,
Senecan Federation Division of Intelligence.
Faction: *Senecan Federation*

Valkyrie
Artificial. Prevo counterpart to Alex Solovy.
Faction: *Independent*

EARTH

Seattle

Alex stared at the array of screens organized neatly above the low table. The whirlwind aftermath of the final battles against the Metigen fleet having at last subsided, it was surely time to go back to work.

She tried and failed to choose any particular screen on which to focus. Her vision blurred as her mind drifted….

Understand you are but a glint, a faint spark in the sea of stars of the true cosmos. Aurora was born but yesterday. Your species only moments ago.

Fifty-one lobbies. Fifty-one subordinate portals, mirrored fifty-one times over in an elaborate, interlocking tunnel network. Fifty-one universes.

We have explained to them that Aurora displays the potential to deliver the very answers we seek, but they are no longer listening.

What answers? To what questions?

We cast you adrift to do as you will, with this one warning: do not come looking for us.

But what were the Metigens *doing*? What purpose drove their universe-tinkering games? She had believed they went to war to preserve the secret of their existence, but what further revelations remained shrouded, hidden beyond those portals?

The Messier 71 job could be interesting, due to the globular cluster's hybrid profile and abnormally high metal content.

Valkyrie's unsolicited input jolted her out of her reverie. She blinked and tried again to concentrate, dropping her elbows to her knees and leaning in closer on the off chance it might help.

Or boring.

"So the Advent contract pays well, but a week sampling asteroids is hardly what I'd call a good time—if that's our first job together you're liable to bolt back to Division before the credits clear the bank. Zwicky Research wants detailed, on-scene readings of the impending supernova WR 102f in the Quintuplet Cluster." She accessed Valkyrie's astronomical databanks.

—*current core 72-80^M*

—*indicators of secondary core collapse*

—*detection of rising levels of Ni_{56} beginning 2322.1215*

"But it's liable to erupt any *day* now. Even I'm not that crazy. There's two planetary scouting jobs, one in NGC 3603 and one in Messier 71, and an initial spectrum survey of two sectors way out in Palomar 1."

A sigh made its way past pursed lips. "What do you think? 3603? I mean, we have to do something, right?"

Her inquiry was met with silence. She gave him a few more seconds then looked over her shoulder.

Caleb stood behind her, as he had for several minutes now. His hands rested on the top of the couch, and he swayed idly back and forth. His gaze appeared to be targeted at the screens displaying her current job offers, but it held no greater focus than hers had a minute ago.

"Caleb? Thoughts?"

He smiled a bit sheepishly. "Sorry. Well...are you sure you don't want to risk the supernova? It could be quite the show."

She peered up at him curiously. His eyes were bright and dancing about. The corners of his mouth were twitching erratically. The corded muscles of his arms flexed beneath rolled-up sleeves as he continued absently fidgeting behind the couch.

"You're going completely stir-crazy, aren't you?"

He sucked his lower lip in to chew on it. "Are you telling me you're not?"

She held his gaze stoically for a beat, then groaned and crossed her arms atop the back of the couch. "I'm about to *crawl out of my skin.*"

He leaned down to tease the tip of his nose against hers. "Want to go climb a mountain and jump off of it?"

"Yes, I do."

ᴁ

PARNES

CAELUM STELLAR SYSTEM, SENECAN FEDERATION SPACE

The mountain loomed with icy temperance over the sheltered valley in the pre-dawn light, casting a ghostly shadow upon the small research camp. Khione, they called it, after the Greek snow nymph.

When Caleb had suggested they go climb a mountain, she had assumed he meant Rainier or McKinley, or possibly some notable peak on Seneca. The fact he had instead meant this frozen volcano on the frozen fourth planet in the Caelum system, a planet so cold it was uninhabitable except in a narrow band at the equator, and then solely by a few dozen planetary geologists and geochemists? It only amplified her appreciation of him. This was fantastic.

It had taken them nearly two days to get here, since she still hadn't managed to acquire the next-generation engine she'd been coveting. Her special use waiver request for the military's highly classified sLume drive continued to be 'under review.' She could steal a copy of the schem flow—okay, she *had* stolen a copy of the schem flow—but she couldn't steal an actual engine, not without getting Valkyrie in trouble with the authorities. Because much to her frustration, Valkyrie now 'officially' belonged to the authorities.

The arrangement, as well as Abigail returning to the service of the Earth Alliance, had been the only way Project Noetica was allowed to continue following the end of the war.

Alex was not in the employ of the government, but she was tethered to it by a thousand intertwined strands. The policymakers argued and dissembled over what to do about Noetica, granting and revoking access to various systems by the Prevos on an almost daily basis. She'd been threatened with house arrest three times and re-location to a top-secret research facility twice...at least twice that she knew of.

Her mother was making a valiant effort to protect her from the worst of the inanity, running interference on countless bureau-cratic meddling and power plays. It was a thoughtful gesture, but one driven by more than merely familial affection. Alex was a single provocation away from flipping everyone off and taking Caleb and her ship wherever the hell she wanted, permanently—something Miriam without a doubt knew.

In point of fact she would have *already* done exactly that, but for the risk to Valkyrie. The Artificial was still housed at EASC and physically under military control. If Alex ran, they could shut Val-kyrie down. They could dismantle her if they wished, which Alex would not allow to occur.

So until she figured out a solution, she nominally played by the government's rules. Rules which, for now, did allow her to roam settled space—so long as she informed the military of her location at all times. *Tethered.*

"The volcano isn't for sport climbing. This is not a tourist des-tination."

Caleb dipped his chin at Dr. Becnel, the research station direc-tor. "We realize it isn't, and we appreciate the serious work you're doing here. That's why we're here as well—work. My companion is a professional interstellar scout, and we were hired to—"

"Oh, I know who you are, both of you. Your faces were all over the news feeds for weeks." The man's glare shifted to her. "Ms. Solovy, I was under the impression you worked in space, however, not planet-side."

They weren't here on a job, of course. Caleb was lying through his teeth, an act he excelled at. Being somewhat less skilled in the art, she gave the man a blank expression. "I'm branching out."

He stared at the two of them for several seconds before shaking his head. "It's your funerals. I can't prohibit you from going up—but I'm also not obligated to come rescue you when you get into trouble. There's more than one breed of dangerous wildlife on Khione, not to mention volatile winds and unstable terrain. The days are lengthy here—you'll have thirty-four Galactic hours of light. But if you're above three thousand meters come nightfall you will freeze to death."

Caleb nodded. "Understood. We'll be careful."

Alex suppressed a laugh as the man wilted beneath the force of Caleb's powers of persuasion.

"We have some backup gear adapted for use in Parnes' conditions in the supply building over there." He pointed out the semitransparent tarp protecting the office from the elements toward the rear of the settlement. "You're welcome to borrow it—after payment of a security deposit equal to replacement value."

Caleb smirked. "A generous offer, but we brought our own equipment."

"Right. In that case, the sun will be up soon, so I suggest you grab your gear and get moving."

ᚱ

"Valkyrie, why does the snow have a faint jade tint to it?"

The Artificial had quickly learned when Alex voiced a question aloud, the response was to be directed to Caleb as well, via a livecomm-style interface they had customized and added to his eVi. It was a habit Alex had worked to develop after some prolonged silences led to awkwardness in the early days of their new living arrangements.

'The planet is rich in the mineral zaratite. The active geology in this region in general and the volcano in particular leads to a constant churning of the zaratite through the atmospheric cycle.'

Caleb shifted his pack as the terrain grew steeper. "It's one reason the scientists are here. The geology is unusually dynamic but fairly stable. The planet's mantle is constantly being expunged and replaced. Though an active volcano under the strict definition, Khione's never experienced a violent eruption. It simply leaks materials from the mantle into the ecosystem to feed the cycle."

She smiled to herself. He'd already known the answer and then some.

He caught her inquiring expression. "Daniel—Isabela's husband—did a stint here a year or so before he died. That's how I knew about this place."

"Ah." She'd finally been able to meet his sister a few weeks earlier when they'd spent several days on Seneca. She'd found Isabela more reserved than her brother, but the woman displayed the same innate charm that made them both easily likeable. Her daughter, on the other hand, had been a whirlwind terror of energy and stream-of-consciousness chatter. Caleb was wonderful with the little girl, however, illuminating yet another facet of his character...one she hadn't expected.

'Also, the ground cover cannot accurately be called snow. Rather, it is a mineralized crystal containing only 4-6% water.'

At least Valkyrie had begun to drop the endless decimal places during normal conversation, Alex observed wryly as she inhaled the dry, frigid air. The atmosphere was breathable but thin, and despite the nanobot injections they'd taken to increase oxygenation in their bloodstreams they'd need to don the breather masks soon.

Caleb glanced behind them and came to a stop. "Turn around."

The research station lay two kilometers down the steep incline. The rays from the white sun, glazed the palest of green hues by the pervasive mineral in the air, now blanketed the valley below. They reflected off the 'snow' to create rainbow prisms upon every surface and lit the settlement in an effulgent glow. Off to the left the ice fields peeked out from Khione's profile in flashes of radiance.

"Well this is sublime, and we're less than halfway up."

"Yep." He massaged her neck through the thermal jacket. "I think if—" His voice cut off with a sharp inhale.

Don't move.

She felt his body tense against her back as first one hand, then the other dropped away.

What is it?

Thirty degrees to our right, eighty meters down the slope. See it?

She honestly didn't. Normal human eyesight discerned only whiteness decorated by the burnished nickel of scattered boulders. So she opened the full connection to Valkyrie, blinked and saw the scene anew.

The creature stood four meters tall even in its crouched stance. Six slender limbs ending in splayed pads were connected by a translucent membrane. No, ten limbs—the filmy membrane continued on to connect to the four appendages currently on the ground. Each pad was lined in a ring of stunted but barbed talons. Its skull was narrow and gaunt, the skin covering it more chitin than flesh. Two front-facing eyes were fixated on them while the additional two eyes located halfway down the long skull darted around in recessed sockets. The color of weathered flint, the creature blended almost perfectly into the surroundings.

I see it.

Do you trust me?

Implicitly.

As soon as I step away, start moving a LOT. If it leaps toward you—which it will—make a show of drawing your Daemon. If it gets too close, don't hesitate to shoot it. Ready?

She mentally noted the precise location of the weapon attached to her utility belt, brought along in case of an encounter with the 'dangerous wildlife.' An encounter like this one, it seemed.

Ready.

His absence manifested in the increased chill at her back. Her left hand went to her hip. She leapt up and waved one arm in the air as her fingers fumbled with the Daemon's clasp through the thermal material of her glove. "Hey you! Over here!"

Her pulse pounded with the force of a hurricane in her ears as the creature sprung forward and the clasp came free. Its upper limbs spread out and the dual membranes became pseudo-wings,

giving it lift as its lower limbs skimmed across the ground at aston-
ishing speed.

She raised the Daemon and pointed it at the creature's thick
chest. Its elongated jaw split apart to expose razored edges and a
spindly, knife-like tongue.

She had no idea where Caleb was, but this beast was ten meters
away and closing fast. She fired.

The laser struggled to penetrate the tough, bony hide. The impact evoked a shrill, strangely hollow cry, but the beast didn't fall
or even slow. She kept the trigger pressed to send an unrelenting
torrent into its chest, albeit to little effect. Her other arm instinctively came up to protect her face and she retreated backward.
Talons extended toward her in concert with the horrifying tongue
and—

—the creature reared up, sending a limb and the attached wing
whizzing by her face. A shimmer flickered to reveal Caleb atop its
spine. His arms wrapped around its skull, and with a violent
wrench he yanked its head up and sideways. It fought him, thrashing wildly as it tried to escape his grasp and throw him off.

Then the left-most eye locked onto Caleb's fierce gaze and the
flailing ceased. Seconds ticked by as they stared unmoving at one
another.

The creature's jaw looked as if it dipped slightly. He gave it a
tight nod in return. In an exaggerated motion he released his hold
and swung off its back to land smoothly on his feet beside it.

Its attention veered to her. She had quit firing, not wanting to
hit Caleb amidst all the thrashing, but the Daemon remained
pointed firmly at its chest.

It took a series of hurried steps to the side until it was able to
watch both of them at once. Its head rose into the air and it let loose
another shrill cry, then pivoted and glided off down the slope.

"Are you hurt?"

She spun to Caleb as he hurried over. "No, it never touched
me." A frown materialized as she willfully tuned Valkyrie's excited

chatter in her head down to a low hum and wiped blood from a cut on his cheek. "You are, though."

He grimaced and wrapped his hand around hers. "Only a scratch, right?"

"I suppose. What just happened?"

"A show of dominance. It respects strength." With a soft exhale he pulled away and slipped his pack off, then dropped it to the ground and began rifling through it. "It's an intelligent animal. Probably not primate-level intelligence, but clearly smarter than most canines and reptiles."

"And you learned how to recognize this...spending your summers roaming the Senecan wilderness as a teenager?"

He shrugged mildly and dug deeper into the pack. "Some of it."

"I didn't know you brought a cloaking shield."

"Habit, and one I'm thinking I'm not inclined to give up." He finally produced two energy bars from the depths of the pack and tossed her one. "Lunch?"

ᴙ

The summit revealed itself in the flood of afternoon sunlight streaming into the broad, shallow caldera. Alex increased the tinting on her goggles and checked the feed to her mask. Even with the supplemental oxygen, her lungs begged for more air, protesting the deepest breaths as inadequate.

The mountainside had served as a bulwark, but now the wind whipped into them with bitter malevolence. Layers of thermal garments designed to capture and amplify the body's natural heat felt as effective as porous gauze in the face of the onslaught.

She drew her hood in tighter. "Fuck it is cold."

"You are the master of understatement, baby. But look...."

She glanced over to find him facing the interior of the volcano. The summit displayed a gently sloping concave exterior. Puffs of jade-white steam shot out of holes in the spongy gray material filling the caldera.

"Whatever. Look at *this*." She gestured in the opposite direction, for the view beyond the summit was nothing short of magnificent.

The research station where they had begun their trek was a tiny speck far below and to the right. In front of them the terrain swept downward to a frozen plain stretching to the horizon. Her initial inclination was to liken it to parts of northeastern Alaska, but this was a decidedly alien landscape.

Jagged fissure rifts split the sheets of ice to allow the same jade-tinged steam to escape into the air, unveiling brilliant emerald crystals beneath the surface. Large swaths of the sheets glowed pale green where the ice grew thin and new fissures would soon form. The sun blazed across the landscape, turning the ice iridescent and filling the sky with daytime auroras.

But for the single dot of humanity in the valley below, it was untouched. Untamed. Nature loosed to run free.

An apt description, I do believe. Does the planet feel alive to you?

It certainly looks *alive, Valkyrie. But peaceful somehow...or at peace with itself. Hopefully it doesn't mind us intruding.*

She dropped her head onto Caleb's shoulder. "You take me to the nicest places."

"I really do. But next week, I'm thinking a sweltering jungle somewhere, full of serpents and flying insects."

"So long as it's warm, I'm in. Though I will point out, a nice, luxurious hot tub overlooking a white, sandy beach is also warm."

"True. And it has other benefits."

Her chuckle sounded reedy in the rarefied air. "I'm temporarily too cold to think about other benefits. Shall we?"

"We shall."

She opened her pack and removed the small glider harness. It consisted primarily of torso-hugging straps attached to a small rectangular module, but when activated the module would unfurl a pair of airfoils. Made of a hyperlight carbon nanofiber, when fully extended and locked open they were strong enough to endure 240 kph winds and a 150 kN impact. Pockets beneath each wing enclosed the hands to provide the wearer a measure of control during the flight, and tensile ankle straps kept their legs from flapping awkwardly and destroying the aerodynamics. But there was no frame, no motor and no brake; the glider was as close to natural wings as humanity had achieved.

They checked the secureness of each other's harnesses, then she grasped his hand and squeezed. "I *love* you."

"Prove it. Fly with me."

Brandishing a spirited grin, she stepped aside to create space for the six-meter span of the gliders. The wings unfurled at her side; she slid her hands into the pockets and felt the material tighten reassuringly. She nodded.

"3...2...1...Go!"

She took a deep breath and leapt.

The second of free fall ticked by in a thousand transcendent nanoseconds. The rush of vertigo spinning her stomach. The stronger rush of wind forcing its way past her layers of clothing to bite into her skin like needles of ice. The feeling that she could fall forever as frozen land and endless starshine rushed past her vision in a blur.

The rush.

For an instant the force of Valkyrie's exhilaration had overwhelmed her thoughts—had come dangerously close to overwhelming her actions. She blinked and reasserted her own will into the forefront.

Keep on like that and you'll let us plummet to our death.

Perhaps I became carried away by the experience.

We need to talk about you and your 'perhapses'—later.

Alex spread her arms, and with a reassuring jolt the wings locked...and she was soaring.

Now, isn't this better?

There was no response.

Valkyrie?

I find I am at a loss for words.

Finally.

A shadow grew overhead as Caleb crossed above her. It had been years since she'd used a glider, and she tweaked the wings a couple of times before finding the proper adjustment to gain altitude and draw up beside him.

Cut it a little close there.

I was in the moment.

He shook his head, but thankfully let her off the hook. They veered to the left, leaving Khione behind to sail above the fullness of the plains.

From above, the sunlight roused the emerald ice into sparkling a fiery, brilliant green. Any imperfections in the tundra vanished as it washed out to a pure white. If only the sun on her back held any warmth whatsoever, it would be perfection.

She laughed in delight as an aurora swirled beneath them, its elusive rays seemingly just out of reach.

Her focus on the colorful show, she didn't notice they had company until she glanced in Caleb's direction—she instinctively jumped in surprise, which very nearly sent her tumbling through the air. She jerked her arms level and kept them stiff until the wings stopped teetering.

An animal, the same breed as the one that attacked them, flew barely fifteen meters beyond him. It maintained an altitude and speed to match their own.

Jesus!

It's okay.

Caleb tilted his head in her direction. She looked to her right as two additional creatures banked in to take up positions beside her.

What are they doing?

We're no longer prey. I think they're saying 'hi.'

Here in the air, they projected a far less ferocious and far more graceful manner than one had on the ground. The membranes turned out to serve as true wings, and the extensive connections meant all their limbs were pulled up into the span, giving them an appearance closer to an ocean ray than a many-limbed reptile.

Valkyrie's voice took on a high-minded tenor in her head. *A reminder that danger can often be disguised by beauty, and beauty by danger.*

She rolled her eyes. *Thanks for the insight, Confucius.*

I was talking about you.

Smartass.

Well, yes.

The creatures accompanied them for another several seconds before dipping lower and slowing. As she checked behind her to confirm they were departing, she noticed dark streaks of discoloration and an open wound on the chest of the one that had first joined Caleb.

It was the same one they had confronted on the ascent. *I'll be damned.*

She murmured a quiet gasp of wonder and exhaled against the wind. With the next breath in she allowed the sensations to consume her fully. This freedom, this embracing of the wild unknown and meeting it on its own terms…this was her life. Now, this would be their life.

She acknowledged the quiet voice in the recesses of her mind, the one whispering it was all a lie—all a contrived creation by its masters beyond the portal—and put it aside for later. Its refrain had become a common one, but it could wait a while longer.

Far in the distance the terrain began to darken into the rocky, uneven crags they had flown past on the way to the village.

We should start descending.

Agreed.

As one their wings dipped, and the icy expanse rose to greet them.

The sensation of motion, of *velocity*, returned as the ground sped by, and it occurred to her she was moving rather fast and the ground looked rather hard and unforgiving. She rotated her shoulders to create drag on the wings—too much, her altitude dropped precipitously. She decreased the angle. Better.

Down there.

They aimed for a wide area of unbroken ice. When the surface was two meters below and her speed had slowed sufficiently, she drew her arms in and disengaged the wings' locks. Her feet hit the ground at a run; then abruptly she was tumbling head over heels. After many bruising revolutions she lurched to a stop lying on her back. Yep, definitely hard *and* unforgiving.

A heavy thud signaled Caleb's arrival to her left.

"Owwww...."

She was laughing, raggedly and in mild exhaustion, as he crawled over and collapsed beside her. When she decided she was capable of movement she tugged her mask off and shifted to rest on his torso. Then she shoved his own mask off and kissed him zealously, high on adrenaline and oxygen and adoration.

He tried to wrap his arms around her, which led to their unfurled wings getting tangled in one another, which led to a more fulsome state of entanglement. Which worked out fine.

She giggled against his lips. "That was spectacular."

"It was. Should cure our restlessness for at least a week."

"Maybe even two..." her eyes gleamed in only partially feigned playfulness "...but what then? What's next? Dare that supernova to erupt on us?"

He regarded her intently. "You know what's next. The sooner you say it, the sooner we can get started."

Her protest lodged in her throat. Of course she knew. She'd known for weeks; part of her had known from the moment she sent the Metigen fleet slinking home.

"We're going back through the portal."

"Damn right we're going back through the portal."

"I mean, what are all those other universes? Are they like ours? Why were they created? What game are the Metigens playing? What are they—"

His mouth smothered hers to halt her rambling, and it was some time later when they came up for air.

She crossed her arms on his sternum and propped her chin up. "We should probably get married before we go. I doubt they'll have the necessary bureaucracy on the other side."

"Excellent point." He had managed to untangle his left arm and reached up to softly caress her cheek. "We should. Let me check my calendar...two Fridays from today looks free."

"Does it now. Okay, February 2nd it is."

"I like this plan. And I suspect there are a few other things we'll need to take care of before we leave."

"A few." Her mind was already racing around the implications. Valkyrie was the biggest source of complications, but she'd also need to find a way to obtain the new engine and...his chest rumbled beneath her as he started chuckling. "What?"

"You're as happy as a kid on Christmas morning right now, aren't you?"

"Unh!" She punched him lightly in the shoulder and rolled off onto the ice. It was late afternoon in the daylight cycle, and the auroras flitted with increasing luminance above them.

"So, um, how do we get back to the *Siyane*?"

"We walk."

"You're kidding."

"I am." He wrangled his pack off and repositioned it to serve as a pillow. "I contacted Dr. Becnel as soon as we landed and humbly requested a pickup, noting we weren't technically on Khione any longer. Somebody will be along in a vehicle. Eventually."

"Terrific." She curled her hands behind her head and stared up at the sky. "We can start planning while we wait. First, we'll need...."

FOUR MONTHS LATER

EARTH

EASC HEADQUARTERS

The gleaming façade shone in the late morning sun, radiant and glittering in a way only newness could exhibit. Tiers of steel and glass rose in staggered, winding levels to soar into the sky. A work of functional art, the offset floors allowed for both gardens and landing pads to blend seamlessly into the design of the structure.

It was, Miriam had to concede, a far more attractive building than the one it replaced.

Construction of the new EASC Headquarters Tower had been completed while she was away. It didn't officially open for business until the next day, but most of the equipment and furnishings had already been transferred from the temporary quarters in the Logistics building, and her new office reputedly awaited her presence.

She almost walked in the entrance brandishing a smile. Luckily she realized her error at the door and donned a stern countenance.

A lieutenant sat behind the front desk testing the functionality of a control panel, but on spotting her he leapt to his feet with a salute. "Admiral Solovy! Welcome, ma'am. We were told you wouldn't arrive until tomorrow. Allow me to show you to your suite."

"I assume I take the center lift until it goes no higher, correct?"

"Um, that does sort of cover it. But—"

"Then I shall show myself up, Lieutenant."

"Yes, ma'am."

Beginning tomorrow there would be two additional security checks between the lobby and the top floor, but this trip required solely her personal security code. She stepped off the lift into a bright, open atrium. The marble floor felt suitably firm beneath her feet; the secretary's station loomed with appropriate intimidation over prospective guests.

Beyond the atrium was her office. She entered her security code a final time and stepped inside.

The desk she'd ordered had arrived ahead of her, as had the matching shelves. Everything had arrived, down to the white-silver tea set she'd purchased a few days earlier. Her favorite visual of David, Alex and herself—taken in 2298 on the lawn of their home in San Francisco—was even loaded into the display atop the desk.

The chair wasn't new, for she'd become accustomed to the one she'd claimed in Logistics. She eased into it and spun slowly around—then was quickly back on her feet and moving to the window.

Except it wasn't a window; it was a door. She had a garden.

Well, perhaps 'garden' was stretching the term a bit. She had a patio decorated in shrubs, flowering morning glories, astilbe and a small table with two chairs.

Beneath her the entirety of the EASC complex spread out. Tiny forms scurried about from one building to the next, and in the distance ships landed at and departed from the spaceport with ordered regularity. Ahead of her the waters of the Strait crashed against the parapets.

Well. This was simply lovely.

"I heard you were in the building."

She turned and motioned Richard out onto the patio. "I only just arrived."

"Word travels fast, especially when it's in panic. They were expecting you tomorrow, I believe."

She draped her arms atop the railing as he joined her. "I wanted to get settled in while it was still quiet. We'll see how the practicality holds up under duress, but I have to say so far I'm pleased."

Richard chuckled lightly. "I won't tell anyone."

"Thank you."

"How was Romane? More to the point, how was your first vacation in…ever, was it?"

"Not *ever*, merely the last decade…or two. And it was very relaxing. That's what vacations are supposed to be, right? Relaxing?"

"That's the rumor."

She nodded. "Then yes, it was relaxing."

"Did you spend the entire visit meeting with the governor and her administration?"

"Only half the visit. I also toured several art galleries, attended a horrifically tawdry circus performance and spent a great deal of time…not worrying."

"Otherwise known as relaxing."

"Yes." She straightened up from the railing but kept her hands atop it. "And now it is time to get back to work."

"Much of the unrest on the hardest-hit colonies has eased with the improvements in services. Now it's mostly squabbling over what to build next, where and for who's favor."

"What about the Order of the True Sentients?"

Richard grimaced. "They will be a problem, I fear. They're extremely well-funded, and we haven't yet managed to find out by whom or what. But after all we've faced, they and their ilk seem like pests rather than real trouble."

"I gave the subject some thought while I was...relaxing. We confronted the greatest threat to our existence humanity has ever seen, and we defeated it. But a year ago we couldn't see it coming; our most skilled forecasters could never have predicted it. What else is out there on the horizon that we can't see?"

She shifted to lean against the railing and meet his gaze more directly. "You and I know the true extent of what Alex and Caleb discovered beyond the portal. I fear we've seen but a small glimpse of the dangers which may await us—dangers for which we are woefully unprepared."

"Granted. So?"

"So, I intend to see to it that we get ourselves prepared. We can't sit on our laurels and be caught unaware a second time."

"True enough. I'm glad the task is in such capable hands."

"Flatterer."

"I'm trying to hone my skills. Speaking of, have you seen Alex recently? I haven't talked to her in a few weeks."

"We had a nice dinner before I left for Romane, in fact. She and Caleb have been on Seneca the last week or so helping his sister move into a new place, but I believe they are headed to Atlantis to meet Kennedy and Noah for a long weekend."

"Good. I'm glad they—"

Miriam held up her hand to silence him. She stared at the message that had come in, searching for the correct reaction. Anger? Fear? Pride? Exasperation?

She settled on the last one, went to the little patio table and sank down in one of the chairs.

"Miriam, what is it?"

She shook her head and laughed. "I'm going to kill her."

At Richard's questioning look she called him over and projected the message to an aural.

ATLANTIS

INDEPENDENT COLONY

Kennedy sighed in contentment and curled up against Noah's chest. The sun's rays streaming in through the open windows warmed her bare skin, and she kicked the sheet off so as to give the rays more fulsome access. "Mmm...can we not leave this room today? Or even the bed?"

Noah's chest rumbled beneath her in a soft chuckle as he played with her hair. "We've got drinks, so we're set there. Eventually we'll need food, but this is why room service exists. So yeah, I think we're good. Who needs sun and sand and surf when we have *this*."

"Not me. Besides, we have sun—and we can see the sand and surf, should we manage to approach the windows."

"I'll take your word for it." His hand trailed lazily down her back, evoking a pleasant murmur from deep in her throat.

"Alex and Caleb will be here today...sometime. They would probably appreciate it if we put clothes on."

"Probably. Have you heard from them yet? I'd like a little warning, say, three or four hours, so I can...." She shuddered beneath his hand as it drifted lower.

"Not yet. I'm sure they got distracted by—" As if on cue, a message from Alex arrived in her eVi. She opened it with only a fraction of her attention, the rest being occupied by Noah's increasingly roving hands.

Then she bolted upright in the bed. "I'm going to kill her. I mean it this time. I am well and truly going to kill her."

Noah raised up on one elbow. "They're not coming?"

She rolled her eyes at the ceiling and flopped onto her back with a groan. "No. No, they are not. And you won't believe where they *are* heading."

◠

SIYANE

METIS NEBULA

The *Siyane* hovered in the thick nebular clouds at the edge of the clearing, out of sight of the Alliance and Federation vessels patrolling the perimeter.

The portal was closed, occupying an invisible point at the center of the empty void in the heart of the Metis Nebula. Its activation would give the watching ships an extra few seconds to prepare for their destruction of any alien vessel that might emerge. The patrols gave the area a wide berth lest they get caught in the explosion of metal and plasma which would accompany such activation.

A few modifications had been made to the *Siyane* in the months since the Metigen War ended. For one, the cockpit had been rearranged a bit. Caleb's chair received an upgrade, hers moved to the left, and they occupied their seats as equals. Many of the sensors and scientific equipment received upgrades as well and now included a number of new features.

They had even made room for Caleb's bike down in the engineering well. It turned out Division secured it after Volosk's murder as part of the crime scene, at first as evidence then later for safekeeping. And who knew? They may need it. On a planet's surface, perhaps. Or on a space station....

Oh, and there was Valkyrie.

It hadn't taken long for the combined processing power of three Artificials enhanced by the neural imprints of some damn clever humans to result in a host of technological leaps. The list of ways they were changing the world was long, but most relevantly for the *Siyane* was the radical miniaturization of quantum boxes and hardware circuitry. What once filled a large room now fit between the interior walls and bulkhead of a small ship.

Abigail had protested the final stage in her loss of Valkyrie, contending she needed the Artificial to assist in the rebuilding of Meno, and in the rebuilding of a human brain. But while quantum communications were able to span the universe—this universe—in an instant, they could not penetrate the portal. Alex needed Valkyrie with her where they were going. She had of course kept that detail to herself, instead arguing the need to get Valkyrie out from under government control.

A compromise had been reached which, while very expensive, did have the benefit of at least partially satisfying the bureaucrats as well: a complete copy of Valkyrie was constructed and an image of her neural net flashed to the new machine.

From the time the new Artificial was activated, it and Valkyrie began diverging, and in a matter of weeks they could no longer be considered the same in any meaningful way. Valkyrie professed no misgivings about the situation, explaining that she intended to view her mirrored copy like a sister. In fact, she was somewhat enamored with the notion of having a sibling; as Alex was an only child it would be a wholly new experience for her.

Caleb grasped Alex's hand in his, and she stood to join him at the viewport. After a moment she halfway faced him, eyes dancing in delight to match his own. "Ready to see what's out there, Mr. Solovy?"

"Hell, yes, Mrs. Marano. Beyond ready. Show me this supposed 'adventure.'"

"Knowing we won't die simply by going through doesn't take the adventure out of it?"

He wrapped an arm around her waist and yanked her closer for an ardent, tantalizing kiss which ended far too soon, then murmured against her lips. "No, it does not. Now let's do this."

She reluctantly disentangled from his embrace to ensure all the systems were in order. "Valkyrie, how about you?"

'You are taking me to explore other universes. I am ready.'

"Okay, then."

The aliens had asserted no one should ever come looking for them—but she had never agreed to that particular term of surrender.

She reached down and sent the gamma signal.

The ring exploded outward to fill with the still mysterious, luminescent plasma. Around it the patrolling ships reacted the next instant, rushing to take up a defensive formation.

Her hand slid across the HUD to the thrusters. With a touch she gunned the impulse engine to full power and accelerated into the portal.

R

AURORA THESI (PORTAL PRIME)

ENISLE SEVENTEEN

I considered the form lying inertly in the stasis chamber.

It appeared a stranger to me. I felt no kinship, no attachment to the body providing my life force. Memory my aspect, I no longer recalled having resided within it. Even so, logic and the reality of Katasketousya origins dictated I once did so.

To find oneself bound inside the confines of a small, frail body, rendered hapless by its myriad limitations, was anathema to me. I moved the stasis chamber into the deepest corner of the structure. The life support system was designed to function for perpetuity without my intervention. Unseen, it would trouble me no further.

I left the structure and its refuge behind to hover at the shore of my lake, finding myself uncertain of what to do next.

Exile.

Such had been the verdict of the Idryma Conclave. Exiled from their ranks in name, title and consciousness. Exiled from Amaranthe. My body retrieved from the *krypti* and relinquished to the dirt of Aurora Thesi.

A watcher with no subjects.

An Analystae with no dominion.

It would be far simpler if it were such a simple matter as this. But my task extended well beyond the rigid strictures of the Idryma. Aurora had been entrusted to me because I understood our purpose more deeply than anyone, save possibly Lakhes.

Histories. Futures. What was inevitable, and all that was not.

The Conclave called Aurora a failure. We would refocus our efforts on the other Enisles, Lakhes proclaimed, in the search for new and innovative prospects. We would try again, Hyperion declared, but ensure firmer restraints were in place from the beginning this time.

To invest time and effort in such an endeavor was foolish, risking all while invalidating the experiment from its inception. Interference may be acceptable in the other Enisles—but not in Aurora, whether this incarnation or any future one. No, the sole path to the answers sought was to serve as Clockmaker Gods, to create the universe then let it become what it dared. But Hyperion's clumsy meddling had demonstrated a lack of understanding of this most fundamental notion.

The answers, I believed, still resided in Aurora. For what the Conclave was too insular to see—or too fearful to admit if they did see—was this: the uprising by the Humans had in fact proven the validity of the principal thesis underlying Aurora's existence. Now was not the time to recoil as mettle failed.

This was the kairos. This was what we had *wanted*. The others might flinch and turn away, but I would not.

I extended, diffusing out over the lake and above the mountains. I was truly alone on Thesi now, as neither Hyperion nor any others would be venturing by to consort with an exile. I was truly alone in spirit now, my consciousness denied entry into the Idryma.

Before departing Aurora for the last time, representatives of the Conclave had placed spatial triggers at the Metis Portal, designed to pitch the apparatus into a dimensional singularity upon its opening from the other side. It had been a near thing, our—their—decision to refrain from destroying the portal immediately.

Only my most elegant arguments had convinced the Conclave they need not permanently foreclose this avenue. Katasketousya appreciated the concept of 'forever' better than most species, and when presented with the alternative of the spatial triggers Lakhes had eventually been persuaded to not take such irrevocable action.

But the Conclave, eager to be rid of the troublesome Aurora and its equally troublesome Analystae Mnemosyne, had perhaps not paid sufficient attention to the details.

I was and had always been the First Analystae of Aurora. This meant I controlled all the apparatuses of the Enisle, observational and otherwise.

The triggers had been deactivated. I could rearm them at any time, and should it become necessary—should the Humans or their scions attempt to launch an armada through the Metis Portal, one bent on wanton destruction of whatever they found—I would do so, regrettably but without hesitation.

But I was the First Analystae of Aurora, and this experiment was not over. Once a proud member of an underground resistance, I was now a rebel from the rebellion.

As the sea spread out beneath me, an alert transmitted the opening of the Metis Portal. I halted far above the waters and waited.

What emerged from the portal was not the feared armada. Instead, it was a single ship. A familiar ship. I felt a quickening in my atoms.

Clever, dangerous girl. I have been expecting you.

VENATORIS

VENATORIS

AN
AURORA
RHAPSODY

SHORT STORY

G. S. JENNSEN

Humanity may have colonized much of the galaxy, but space remains as dangerous as ever, and so do the people inhabiting it.

When Alexis Solovy—space explorer, freelance scout, recalcitrant wanderer—lands the contract of a lifetime, the race is on to claim the prize. Now she must not only outrun but outsmart her rivals to uncover the secrets of an ancient, mysterious pulsar. For deep in the void, far beyond the reach of civilization, wealth and renown matter little absent the ultimate reward: survival.

Set five years before *STARSHINE: Aurora Rising Book One (Amaranthe #1)*, *Venatoris* takes a younger, wilder, rough-around-the-edges Alexis Solovy and Kennedy Rossi on an unforgettable adventure across the stars.   '

*

Venatoris is the most fun I've ever had writing a short story, and some of the most fun I've had writing, period. It's a wild, rollicking space adventure starring Alex Solovy, Kennedy Rossi, and Bob. Who's Bob? You'll see.

Venatoris takes place after Restless I *and five years before* Starshine. *While your enjoyment of it can only increase the better you know Alex and Kennedy, it can be enjoyed at any time.*

DRAMATIS PERSONAE

Alexis 'Alex' Solovy

Starship pilot, scout and space explorer;
daughter of Miriam and David Solovy.
Faction: *Earth Alliance*

Kennedy Rossi

Ship Designer, IS Design;
friend of Alex Solovy.
Faction: *Earth Alliance*

Bob Patera

Starship pilot and space scout.
Faction: *Independent*

Joaquin Kyril

Starship pilot and space scout.
Faction: *Independent*

"The fast lane I am flying down is one
with no end in sight
filled with reckless adventure and
paved with dangerous delights."

— *Ashley Young*

2317
(5 YEARS BEFORE THE EVENTS OF STARSHINE)

YUZHOU LI ORBITAL STATION

SHI SHEN STELLAR SYSTEM
1,080 PARSECS FROM EARTH

"Double bourbon, straight up. Double everything. Except the ice. Don't double the ice."

Alexis Solovy glanced down the bar in idle curiosity at the source of the dramatic pronouncement. A woman with frizzy black hair and pale, bleached skin sagged off a stool and onto the bar, arms splayed out in defeat. She looked familiar, but damned if Alex could pull a name out of anywhere. "Bad day?"

The woman didn't lift her head from where it lay propped sideways on her elbow. "My ship is trashed. A mangled heap. Bloody asteroid spun out when I tried to grapple it. I limped back here like a crippled monkey, jack shit to show for my trouble."

Alex raised her glass in contrived sympathy and turned away. If the woman didn't have any useful leads, it wasn't worth the pain of engaging in conversation, polite or otherwise.

Intel was the only reason to come to this godforsaken place, the sleaziest bar on the sleaziest space station for two kiloparsecs. Tidbits. Information. Leads. On a good night, contracts.

Her eyes roved over the room in search of better prospects. The bar was nearly two-thirds full—loud and busy, but not so full as to preclude card and target games and the occasional display of bra-vado. Bad synth blaring out of the speakers made it feel rowdier than the reality.

Alex knew half the people on sight. Some she was on a last name basis with; others, an epithet basis. Many were interstellar scouts, freelance—same as her, while a few were traders, smugglers, or both. But she didn't see any corp reps or brokers. Was no one in this cursed place doing business?

"Alex, doll, you need something stronger than...what *are* you drinking?"

She leveled an unimpressed scowl in Bob Patera's direction as he leaned on the bar beside her. "A Carina Nova. They make it in civilized places like Earth. Luckily, the bartender's visited civilized places."

He nodded with as much vigor as his inebriated state allowed. "Still need to get you something stronger."

"Can't. I'm working."

He stared at her skeptically but couldn't seem to think of a suit-able response. Finally he took a long, fulsome sip of his drink, a dark and frothy concoction. "Go on a date with me."

It had to be at least the seventy-fourth time he'd asked in the two and a half years since she'd met him. "No."

"Why not?"

"Because you think you're a space pirate, Bob."

"But I am a space pirate."

She laughed in spite of herself. "My point exactly."

"You dated that Ethan Tollis guy, and he thinks he's a synth star."

"He *is* a synth star." And the dating happened years ago, before Ethan found well-deserved fame, but she wasn't inclined to correct him.

He looked genuinely offended. "I am a space pirate."

Patera was a good guy; a functioning drunk and a righteous lech, but a good guy nonetheless. He took the odd scouting job mostly to entertain himself and to have tales to brag about at any of a staggering variety of bars, of which this was only one.

"Oh, clearly. But—"

She recognized the man the instant he stepped in the bar and made sure she was the first person he made eye contact with. "Sorry, Bob, got to go. Working."

The man sat down at a table in the corner near the door. She stood up and headed for it with an air of deliberate casualness. It wouldn't do for anyone else to notice him and beat her there, but she also didn't want anyone else to notice her running for him.

She made it to the table scot-free and slid in opposite him. "You have a job?" Perhaps not the smoothest greeting, but she rarely had the patience for pleasantries.

He didn't appear to mind. As a respected and experienced broker for numerous Alliance corps, he presumably knew interstellar scouts weren't always the most socially well-adjusted people.

"Astral Materials is getting ready to post an open contract for rare, high value elements at a newly discovered pulsar in Messier 71."

Messier 71 lay a considerable distance from Shi Shen, out in the void beyond settled space. She was okay with that.

"What's special about it?"

"It's a millisecond pulsar with three suspected planets identified. The scientific data is so promising they already gave it a name: Shanshuo. It's the Chinese word for—"

"Scintillation. I know. And it's an open contract?"

"Should hit the boards in the next hour or so. You did a great job on the contract for Palaimo last month, so I thought you'd be interested in a little forewarning."

Pulsar planets were rare, and rare was interesting. Better yet, millisecond pulsars were very, very old, which meant lots of opportunities for elements to bake, mature and transform. The odds leaned toward something lucrative waiting at Shanshuo.

She harbored no doubts she would find that something if it was there to find, but she also had to find it *first*. "What's the payout?"

"Depends on what you find."

Her gaze bore into him until he made a hedging motion. "200K to 1.2 million."

She managed to stand up without sending the chair skittering across the floor. "Appreciate the tip."

Then she slinked out the door, hoping no one noticed her exit, and hurried down the curving walkway of the station's outer torus as she messaged Kennedy.

Ken, where are you? It's time to quit partying and start working.
The response took several seconds to come in.

Are you sure? I literally just met a delicious merchant from Arcadia. He sells custom wide-band decrypters fabbed onsite.

And he needs you to come to his hotel room so he can show them to you?

Actually I suggested the hotel room.
Alex reached the transfer lift and hopped aboard as it departed.

Hey, it's your vacation, but you said you wanted to come on a job with me so you could, and I quote, 'See what I did with all my free time.' Here's your chance. You can stay and bed Don Juan if you want, but I'm clamps off in twenty.

Oh, fine. I'll meet you at the ship. I've got to disentangle myself here. Twenty, Ken.

ᴙ

The hangar deck did not look to be in compliance with any safety regs from this century, and certainly not Earth Alliance regs, which Shi Shen claimed to be subject to. Maybe the jurisdiction got fuzzy once one breached space? Alex knew better, though. Her mother—Queen Admiral of the Universe, Earth Alliance Strategic Command Division—would have an apoplectic fit if she saw the wreck this place was. But her mother did not deign to frequent places such as this.

A third of the bays were filled with half-broken ships while their owners, bots and assorted mechanics tried to put them back together. Two men were busy installing a new impulse engine in the ship next to hers, right there on the deck. She shook her head and strode past them.

The *Siyane* sat at the end of the left row. Sleek, aerodynamic lines gleamed panther black, giving it a predatory appearance. It wasn't the largest ship in the bay, but by God it was the most beautiful. As well it should be, since she'd designed it herself. Built to spec by the company Kennedy worked for, it represented nothing short of perfection.

...Except for all the upgrades and customizations she desperately wanted to make but could not yet afford. *Step by step, day by day.*

Kennedy came rushing up behind her, a mess of golden curls bouncing around a flushed face as she repositioned the straps of her jade slip dress on her shoulders. She skidded to a stop in a huff. "You're not on board yet? I could've gotten—"

"You can tell me on the way, Ken. Come on."

"Where are we going?"

"On an adventure. Trust me, it'll be fun."

SIYANE

MESSIER 71
PSR J1952+1846
4,220 PARSECS FROM EARTH

Many people believed humanity's mere presence in the stars beyond its home planet had rendered space civilized.

Superluminal travel allowed them to hopscotch over the void on their way from one colony to the next. Half the time they didn't even bother to glance out a ship's viewport and note it was the *stars* they journeyed through.

But out here, twelve hundred parsecs from the nearest settled world—which happened to be the most uncivilized world of them all, run by gangsters, murderers and thieves—space revealed its true nature. Vast. Untamed. Dangerous.

In other words, her playground.

Alex noted all this with a brief smile of anticipation as she increased the thrust of the impulse engine and accelerated into the stellar system hiding in a far corner of Messier 71. Not the venue for idle musing.

The race was already on. Word of the contract had spread across the width and breadth of the freelance scout network by now, and she'd be deluding herself if she thought she'd be able to close this deal without competition.

The rules for claiming 'property' in unexplored, unowned space were straightforward: plant a beacon at the location detailing the extent of the claim and the name of the claimant. Once the broadcast reached the relevant authorities—a matter of seconds—the claim was certified. Period, full stop. It was the only practical way to handle development of the forty billion star systems still unexplored in their little corner of the galaxy.

The various governments generated much to-do about their new discoveries. Corporations, however, simply took what they wanted.

Well, it would be more accurate to say corporations paid people to find and claim what they wanted for them. People like her....

"Oh, *chyertu.*" Alex groaned as the long-range scanner picked up the telltale signs of another vessel in the system. A database check identified the owner of the ship bearing that particular emission signature.

"Problem?" Kennedy muttered as she ascended the spiral staircase from the personal quarters below wearing far more appropriate sweats and a tee.

"Joaquin Kyril's here."

Her friend leaned against the cockpit half-wall and crossed her arms over her chest. "Who?"

"Asshole extraordinaire. Not a scintilla of hunter skills to his name. He wouldn't recognize a neutron star glitch if it sauntered up and slapped him across his peevish face."

Kennedy's eyes narrowed in contemplation. "Wait, is he that guy we bumped into on Demeter last year? He was cute."

"Really, Ken? I offer a string of insults by way of introduction, and you go straight to 'cute'?"

"I didn't say he was nice or upstanding. Just said he was cute. I can't believe you haven't put a second chair in the cockpit yet. Where am I supposed to sit?"

Alex shrugged. "The floor? The couch back in the main cabin? You're the only person who ever comes out with me."

"What about Malcolm?"

She snorted. "We're nowhere near the stage where he goes with me...anywhere that isn't on Earth. Seriously, he hasn't even seen my bedroom."

"Here on the ship or at your apartment in San Francisco?"

"Either." She'd been on two dates with Lt. Col. Malcolm Jenner in the past month; the third might have happened this week, were she not out here in the void. Perhaps it would happen next week, if she didn't die out here in the void.

He wasn't her type. For one, he was military—a Marine of all things—which she'd been swearing off since...since a long time. He was upstanding and proper and gentlemanly to a cringe-inducing fault.

But he was also smart, considerate and funny in a self-effacing way. And handsome, even if he did have to keep his hair shorn in an annoying military close-crop. For reasons she hadn't yet found the words to articulate, she liked him. Maybe. She'd worry about it later. Right now she had to work.

Kyril wandered around five AU out from the pulsar...searching for the outermost planetary body? If so, he was searching in the wrong place.

Shanshuo hadn't been receiving scientific attention long enough for the eccentricity to be accurately measured, but the orbit appeared wildly erratic. Kyril was guessing.

Alex studied what data existed on the sequential orbits of the third body.

ORBIT 1: *Inclination: 12.3°; Ω: 147°; Period: 3.8 years*
ORBIT 2: *Inclination: 17.6°; Ω: 132°; Period: 4.1 years*

ORBIT 3: *Inclination: 9.5°; Ω: 153°; Period: Incomplete (859 days as of yesterday)*

She ran through some calculations then killed all the screens to stand and stare out the viewport.

They weren't able to *see* the pulsar, of course, as it emitted primarily X-rays. A spectrum filter engaged over the viewport to rectify the deficiency in their eyesight.

"Ooh, that's pretty."

"In a manner of speaking." Like a lighthouse on an *ampaKhat* high, the X-ray beam spun madly, strobing across the viewport faster than she could blink. It was hypnotizing, and she let it cast its spell. She watched without seeing as her vision blurred under the mesmerizing rhythm.

There.

She dropped back into the cockpit chair, strapped in and set a course for *there*.

ℛ

Cold gas giant, 0.8 the size of Jupiter, sporting a standard hydrogen and helium composition. Likely a captured planet, although with an orbit this close it must have been falling into Shanshuo for billions of years. Still, gas giants, whether cold, room temperature or hot, ranked among the most common non-stellar bodies in the galaxy.

"Ugh. Boring."

Kennedy now sat on the floor, propped up against the wall eating roasted almonds. "Are you kidding? Look at those colors, at the way the clouds swirl together. This planet is spiffing art."

She didn't disagree, but…. "I know, but we're not here for art. We're here to find elements worth money to Astral Materials, and as lovely as this planet may be, it's not lucrative. One day I'll have earned sufficient credits to be able to spend days gaping in wonder at such sights, but that day isn't today."

"I'm sorry, I didn't mean…."

She spared Kennedy a quick, closed-mouth smile. "And I didn't either." Kennedy, or more specifically her family, was wealthy beyond the numbers to count it, but it hadn't mattered since seven minutes after they'd met as freshmen at university.

With a sigh she started to pull away and shift her focus to the inner bodies when the scanner beeped to inform her of another vessel in proximity.

She glared at the screen incredulously. Kyril was *ghosting* her?

Shit. His ship was faster than hers, one reason she desperately needed the proceeds from this contract. If he could track her, he'd be able to leapfrog her the instant she struck figurative—or possibly literal—gold and sling a beacon. He could steal the discovery out from under her while she watched in impotent fury. And he would do precisely that without a moment's hesitation.

"Dammit, I should have spent last month's money on a real dampener field instead of a new ionized gas analyzer." The dampener field was on the list, but the list was a busy place. And now she floated out here with no way to mask her engine's emission signature and no way to shake Kyril's tail.

"You know, IS Design recently introduced a new prototype dampener field which is nineteen percent more effective at eighty-one percent the power requirements of the previous gen model."

"Did you design it?"

"I helped. A lot, in truth, but I'm still too low on the corporate ladder to get the credit for it." In response to Alex's questioning gaze, Kennedy grinned smugly. "Soon."

"I've no doubt."

Alex pretended to be scanning the planet below, like there might legitimately be something worthy of finding, while she racked her brain for a solution to the problem that was Joaquin Kyril.

It seemed she was not going to be allowed to explore the system, investigating every object for possible valuable elements. She'd only have one real shot at finding and claiming the mother lode.

So where could the mother lode be hiding?

She leaned down and grabbed a handful of Kennedy's almonds. The second suspected planet had, by the timing measurements, a notably strange orbit. She considered it a minute…and palmed her forehead with her free hand.

"I'm an idiot."

"Not usually."

"The second object the researchers detected isn't orbiting Shanshuo. It's orbiting this planet. It probably got brought along for the ride when the gas giant was captured."

"So?"

"So regardless of whether it's a moon, planetoid or true planet, it'll be small and rocky. Small and rocky is—"

"Boring?"

Alex chuckled. "Well, yes. Okay, this leaves the innermost body. It's zipping around at an orbital period of 3.2 hours, which means it's close to the pulsar. Damn close." Dangerously close, at least for a puny little personal scout ship.

She imagined the *Siyane* protesting the insult with an aura of miffed indignation, and apologized silently. It certainly was not puny to her; it was, in point of fact, everything she had ever wanted.

"The type of relationship exhibited here—a tight, rapid orbit in the shadow of the pulsar—pegs it as a companion star rather than a planet. A white dwarf having its matter leeched away by the primary star?"

"Were you directing the question at me? 'Cause I'm an engineer, not a space junkie."

Alex mumbled a distracted reply. White dwarfs were a dime a dozen and as boring as the gas giant. But if it was a true white dwarf, the researchers should've been able to identify it as such relatively easily.

She swung toward Shanshuo in feigned casualness so as not to pique Kyril's interest, tuning out the *voom-voom-voom* strobe of the pulsar in favor of trying to catch sight of the orbiting companion.

She blinked.

There.

Blinked again. Gone.

But it *had* been there, a tiny dot of absence racing across the X-ray light. She readied the spectrum analyzer to take a broad spectrum reading. She'd filter out the pulsar's spectrum signature afterward to reveal the companion's data.

The scanner panned until she relocated it. Fantastic. Effective surface temperature estimated at....

She frowned. "That can't be correct." Either the white dwarf was older than the universe—a dubious supposition—or the pulsar had siphoned off the outer layers completely, evaporating the star and leaving behind naught but its core.

Possibly its exotic carbon diamond-like core? What were the odds?

Vanishingly low, but higher than they had been a few minutes ago and doubtless higher than the first option.

Kennedy stood and peered out the viewport. "What've you got?"

"Maybe, just maybe, something wonderful."

She didn't elaborate for now; she'd been dallying for too long, and Kyril would be getting suspicious. And now she *really* needed a plan.

The small, rocky planet orbiting the gas giant had a thin atmosphere and varied terrain. Terrain she'd be able to lose Kyril in for several seconds at a minimum. Since her in-atmo pulse detonation engine didn't emit an identifiable signature, it might be enough.

"I need help. I need someone else. Who else is here?"

"I'm here."

Alex laughed. "I mean another ship."

Kennedy shrugged and returned to the floor. "Ah. Can't help you then."

The potential payout marked this as an enticing contract, if a marginally risky one. Pulsars didn't qualify as friendly environs for humans. The ionizing radiation alone, not to mention the powerhouse X-ray beacon, meant an early death for anyone not in a strongly shielded vessel.

Luckily for her, she did have those shields. The best radiation shielding last year's money could buy.

She tuned the emission sensor to its farthest range and filtered out the quite noisy pulsar radiation. Kyril's ship showed up immediately, right up her ass, leading her to growl a particularly colorful Russian curse under her breath.

"Your dad teach you that word?"

"Not intentionally."

After another pass two additional dots materialized, which earned another, nearly as colorful exclamation.

Once the targets were pegged, she refined the scanner's parameters until she had definable signatures then fed them into the ship database. The first one didn't match any entries, but the second....

Alex sent a secure comm hail. "Hey, Bob. What brings you to the void today?"

"Solovy? Dammit. Whatever brought me here, I'm not going to get it now, so I might as well turn around, head home and go get plastered."

He wasn't wrong. Bob Patera may be a better scout than Kyril, but that wasn't saying much. "Glad to see you accept the inevitability of my triumph, but don't rush off yet. I've got a proposition for you."

"Be still my heart."

She rolled her eyes. "Simmer down. It's not that kind of proposition. Joaquin Kyril is glued to my ass and I need to ditch him. Help me do that long enough for me to find elements which will satisfy the Astral contract, and you'll get ten percent of the proceeds."

"Fifteen percent."

"Twelve percent."

"Twelve percent and you have a drink with me next week."

She drummed her fingers on the dash. "All right. But a drink means a drink, nothing else."

"Oh, come on. We should at least have sex, if only to get all this sexual tension out of our systems."

Kennedy arched an eyebrow in interest, but Alex shook her head in a vehement *no*. "There is no sexual tension between us, Bob."

"Sure there is."

"Those are your dreams. This is reality. So are you in?"

"Point the way."

She exhaled in relief. "Terrific. You've got a Genyx VII impulse drive, right?"

"I won't ask how you knew that. Yes, the C2 model."

Alex toggled the comm and waved Kennedy up off the floor. "Can you figure out what he needs to do to his engine to make it approximate my emission signature?"

Kennedy nodded and jogged to the data center in the main cabin.

Her outward demeanor made it easy to forget—especially when the woman was in full-on vacation mode—but Ken was smart. Exceptionally smart. And she knew more about all the major components of starships than anyone Alex had met. Odds were she had the specs on the Genyx VII drive memorized, along with the specs for all the other commercial engine models.

Alex switched the comm channel back on. "In a minute I'll send you some adjustments you need to make to the power flow to your engine and a tiny tweak to its negative mass regulator."

"You want me to mutilate my engine?"

"Improve it, actually. You're going to pretend to be me. Once you've made the adjustments, move to the far side of the middle body and wait there until I tell you to come in-atmo. When you get close, I'll go dark. You'll take my place, then bail and get back to the gas giant."

"This body is...where? In case you hadn't realized it, I legitimately meant 'point the way.'"

It wasn't his fault he was a bad scout. Not even a bad scout, really—merely an ordinary one. "It's orbiting the gas giant, inclination 27.6° off the pulsar's reference plane at 1,722 megameters, give or take."

"I can work with that. What are you planning to do once I lead Kyril astray?"

She hesitated. She liked Bob as far as it went, but it didn't mean she trusted him. Not when hundreds of thousands if not millions of credits were at stake. "I'm going to go earn our riches."

Kennedy returned to the cockpit and, at Alex's gesture of approval, input the calculations and sent them to Bob.

"Fine, don't tell me. I'll just fly around jerking off until you decide I can stop."

"What you do on your ship is your own business."

"It most definitely is. Got your instructions. Give me five minutes."

Alex veered around a bit to make it look as if she were chasing down a potential find, shaking her head when Kyril followed like a proselyte. Still, he *had* to be getting suspicious by now. But what was he apt to do? Find anything of value himself?

Abruptly she stood and paced through the main cabin to burn off a fraction of her mounting nerves. She needed razor-sharp reflexes for what came next, not the jitters.

"So, where *are* we running off to once you lose this Kyril guy?"

Alex pointed out the viewport in the direction of the pulsar.

Kennedy canted her head to the side. "Sure. Why not?"

It took six and a half minutes, but Bob reported in. *"I'm on my way to you."*

She returned to the chair in a flash. "I see you. Come in under the planet's profile so he won't pick you up."

"Yep. You truly hate this guy, don't you?"

"Don't you?"

"He's a gilded-spoon prick, no doubt."

"He's a thief. He lets others do the work then finds underhanded ways to steal what he can from them. And he is brutal and unrepentant about it."

"Fair assessment. I guess I don't take it as personally as you do."

One of a thousand reasons why she was better at this than him, and would soon be the best.

Alex accelerated away from the gas giant and toward its satellite, and this time she smirked when Kyril followed behind at some distance. Did he honestly think she didn't know he lurked out there?

The atmosphere turned out to be even thinner than she'd expected. She glanced at Kennedy. "Will the pulse detonation engine operate in this weak of an atmosphere? I mean it should, right?"

Kennedy scrutinized the HUD screen displaying the gas percentages and cringed. "Uh...probably?"

"Good enough." She pointed the nose of the ship down and dove. When the atmosphere began to fight her she reached over and activated the transition from impulse power to the pulse detonation engine. They held their breath.

The ship jerked as the engine struggled for a minute...then began humming quietly.

The meager cloud cover dissipated to reveal a mountainous terrain. Perfect.

She leveled off a kilometer above the surface. "You'll want to strap in to the jump seat."

Kennedy's eyes widened. "Should I get a drink, too?"

"After."

Her face contorted into a grimace as she retreated to the main cabin.

Alex guided the *Siyane* toward the mountains, seeking out a path through the crests and valleys.

Kyril's ship was faster than hers in space; she had to assume it was faster in-atmo as well. But she could fly circles around him in her sleep using nothing but her left pinky. It wasn't arrogance; it was fact.

Perhaps a smidge of arrogance.

She cracked her neck and dipped until she cruised thirty meters from the sloping incline and tilted the belly of the ship toward it. No trees softened the scenery, and boulders rushed past in a blur.

Ahead, a ridge split into a deep fissure, more gorge than valley. She plunged into it, staying close to the ground.

Kyril emerged from the bluffs behind her. He'd drawn far closer, which represented a problem. He must think she was zeroing in on a find.

This gorge was doing nothing for her. She spotted a narrow cleft to the right. Too narrow? *Nah.*

She increased her speed, flipped the ship sideways and slipped into the gap.

"Alex, the hell!"

She gritted her teeth and tried to concentrate on flying. The gap hadn't widened yet. "I did tell you to strap in."

Reluctantly she spared a brief motion to activate the comm channel. "Bob, get down here and head to…33.2° N, 114.1° W." The coordinates lay a hundred kilometers northwest of her current location. It should work.

"I'm not finished yet."

"Bob."

"Right. Heading there now."

Finally the terrain opened up, though the mountains grew far steeper. Jagged spikes jutting up from a dead landscape.

She swerved to the left to dart between two peaks then dropped down as low as she dared.

Kyril's blip followed. Motherfucker.

But it stayed more distant now. He was flying safely. "Coward."

Emboldened, she sped onward, dipping and weaving through the range. When another fissure came into view, she pivoted hard and raced through it, a mite too snugly for comfort. She was glad Kennedy wasn't up here to see how near to the cliff walls they flew.

On the scanner, Kyril slowed almost to a stop, handing her the break she needed. She found a basin on the topography map six kilometers to the northeast.

"Bob, shift to 33.8° N, 113.9° W and get ready."

"Yes, ma'am."

One last corkscrew turn…and….

She decelerated hard and plummeted toward the ground; when ten meters remained she killed the engine. "Now, Bob—17.8° N heading, then get back to space ASAP."

The ship shuddered roughly as it slammed to the ground. A couple of yellow warnings flashed across the HUD, but nothing critical.

"You are one crazy woman, Solovy."

"Thank you. I'm flattered."

Kennedy's voice sounded shaky behind her. "Um, did we crash?"

"Not technically. It's not crashing if it's on purpose."

Kyril had begun moving again and closed in on her location. Alex peered up as he passed overhead, but the paltry light didn't allow her to make out his ship. *Keep going. Keep going.*

He kept going, following Bob's blip into the darkness.

Bob did a surprisingly decent job of picking up where she left off. She was moderately impressed, not as if she'd tell him so.

But if she reengaged the engine too soon, Kyril's scanner might pick up the energy flare.

She breathed in. Out. Waited.

Slowly, cautiously, she lifted off the surface, spun and climbed through the atmosphere in the opposite direction from where Bob had flown.

They exited on the opposite side of the satellite from the gas giant, at which point she had no choice but to run the impulse engine for a minute or so.

"You can unstrap now."

Kennedy stumbled into the cockpit. "Okay, that sucked. What's next?"

Alex didn't answer. Better for her friend not to know until it was already done.

No time to reconsider. She activated the sLume drive and executed a pinpoint superluminal traversal to barely outside the not-a-white-dwarf-not-a-planet's orbit.

The warp bubble had hardly formed around the *Siyane* when it evaporated. Only then did the surge of adrenaline hit her.

A 2.7 AU superluminal trip was not a maneuver one did every day, mostly due to the fact it was dangerous as all hell. If she'd delayed another second—three-quarters of a second—before disengaging the sLume drive, they would've found themselves inside the pulsar. And dead.

"Did you...oh my God, you did. I think I'm...yeah, I'm going to go back to the couch and faint."

Alex grinned a bit wildly. "What? It worked, didn't it?"

"And if it hadn't?"

"We'd never be the wiser."

"Because we'd be vaporized."

"Yes. Now I don't have a lot of time, so hush."

Kennedy nodded weakly and wandered off. "Couch. Fainting. This is the worst vacation ever."

Alex blinked and worked to focus the adrenaline rush on productive endeavors such as catching up to the object, whatever it was, and matching its orbit. Something else guaranteed to be fun, since it was moving *fast*.

At such close proximity the pulsar taxed the radiation shield, but it would hold. She hoped. If this panned out, Astral-owned industrial vessels equipped with far stronger shielding would be able to hang out here for weeks at a stretch, but she couldn't risk staying more than...she checked the diagnostics...twenty-four minutes.

She had a solid bead on the orbital path of the object now, and she accelerated into a parallel trajectory. It gained on her from behind; she continued increasing her speed until she'd matched its velocity and it whisked along a sliver under four megameters off her port.

Trajectory stabilized, she blocked the massive X-ray radiation of the pulsar from the viewport and looked over.

She'd seen many interesting things in her three years of freelance scouting. Beautiful things, terrifying things. She needed a little sleep and a lot of drinks to process what she saw now, but she suspected this topped them all.

"Ken, get up here."

"But I'm still fainting."

"Whatever. Get your ass up here."

The planet-sized body—a quick measurement suggested a 40-50K kilometer diameter—appeared to be composed of a crystalline mineral so clear it was nearly transparent. The sole reason she was unable to see all the way through to the other side was that eventually, thousands of meters below the surface, the inner core darkened into an extremely dense form of carbon. Beyond the brilliance of the outer material, the body retained no more than a trace of natural luminosity. Plainly no longer a white dwarf; not for millennia.

The result of it being stripped of its outer layers then its stellar nature was a surface and outer core which looked a great deal like diamond but was likely something far more precious.

"What...ohhhh." Kennedy brought a hand to her mouth. "This is the most exquisite thing I've ever seen."

"Pretty much."

"You upgraded your radiation shield, right? Because I can get you a next-gen kit for cost."

"Let's do that. Soon as we get back."

Many white dwarfs had carbon-oxygen cores, but humanity thus far lacked the technology to harvest stars. Cold planetoids, on the other hand?

A dozen so-called carbon planets had been stripped bare to minimal riches for companies long forgotten, but only one other true 'diamond planet' had ever been discovered, orbiting the Fyren pulsar. A hundred twenty years ago the Magellan Aeronautics founder had made a fortune and funded an entire generation of interstellar private spacecraft by being the first to reach it and mine it.

Alex jerked out of the reverie. "Crap, the beacon!"

She'd been mooning over the splendor of the singular object speeding alongside them to the point of forgetting her mission. She hurriedly programmed in the details she hadn't known until now and launched it directly at the body.

The beacon plummeted to six kilometers above the ground, then decelerated and adopted a low-altitude orbit and began transmitting to everyone in the galaxy who mattered. Alex sank in her chair with an exuberant cackle.

"Bob, you and I are going to be rich—well, I'm going to be rich. You're going to be slightly more affluent."

Kennedy's face lit up in excitement. "If you're truly earning that much money from this find, I have got so many ideas—"

"Assuming you survive the next few minutes. Kyril just turned tail and made a beeline for the pulsar. Or for you. I'm guessing for you."

Couldn't she spend five seconds enjoying her success in peace? Apparently not.

She straightened up in the chair and began to retreat from the planet. Her shield only had eight minutes worth of full functionality remaining before it started failing. She needed to move to a safe distance, and soon.

"Solovy, you bitch! You think you can get away with such a bullshit scam right in front of me?"

"Nice to talk to you, too, Kyril. Oh, wait. No, it's not. So sorry your plan to ghost then leapfrog me didn't pan out. Better luck next time. Or preferably, worse luck."

"Is that a bloody diamond planet? No. No way are you stealing millions from me. Not this time."

"He wouldn't dare try to shoot you down, would he?"

"Strap back in." She killed the heat and lights in the cabin and diverted the extra power to the defensive shield and increased the distance between her and the pulsar. Another couple of megameters and she'd be distant enough to engage the sLume drive and disappear—

—the *Siyane* shuddered as the laser hit it full-on broadside.

Kennedy's shocked gasp echoed behind her. "That bastard shot at you!"

"Not so cute now, is he?"

The shield held, but it had depleted to thirty-eight percent from the single hit. Kyril had top of the line everything it seemed, including weaponry.

Alex hit the comm. "Goddammit, Kyril, if you shoot at me again you will regret it."

"It would be such a shame if you accidentally got too close to the pulsar and met an unfortunate demise. Astral Materials will mourn your death while they pay me for the contract."

Fuck, no. Not going to happen.

She frantically pulled power from everywhere she could find it to recharge the defensive shield faster, located Kyril on the scanner and locked on.

She returned fire. The laser skimmed off his hull.

Nose down. Fired.

Hard port. Fired again.

She arced above him in a high-g maneuver, firing the whole way.

His shield had to be getting low. Hers had climbed to seventy percent, which was a good thing as he finally managed to track her and return fire. In a flash she was down to nine percent shields....

"Hit him again. I got your back."

Bob arrived out of nowhere above Kyril's ship, bless his drunken soul. She fired once more.

So did Bob.

Hers hit first, but it was Bob's shot that broke through the shield and caught the port rear of the ship. Hard.

The force of the strike sent Kyril's ship hurtling toward Shanshuo in an uncontrolled spin.

No blip on the scanner appeared to indicate the launch of an escape pod or chute as the ship was swallowed up by the pulsar.

Alex threw her arms on the dash and dropped her head onto them.

"Okay, Bob, twenty percent...and two drinks. You earned it."

"I didn't actually mean to kill him."

He sounded almost remorseful; she got that. "He intended to kill *us*. If you try to show mercy to someone like him, they will twist it back on you and use it to destroy you."

"When you put it that way...frankly, in your sultry voice it's kind of hot. Drinks—when and where?"

She sighed in weary amusement. "I'll be in touch. Promise."

When she lifted her head from the dash, Kennedy was standing beside her staring out the viewport. Her hands trembled at her sides. "Is it always like this?"

"Scouting? Nah. Sometimes it's dangerous."

Q&A FOR *VENATORIS*
INCLUDED IN
BEYOND THE STARS: A PLANET TOO FAR

I loved the atmosphere you created in *Venatoris*. We got the "feel" of it right away... the frontier vibe and the scent of unbridled competition. How do you go about envisioning an unknown world in an imaginary galaxy?

All my writing is grounded in the core concept that no matter how much our technology advances, so long as keep these bodies of ours (however heavily augmented) we'll remain fundamentally human. This means whatever we find out there in the stars, we'll see it and experience it through the same human perspective we have now. This allows me to present what are often mind-blowing, nearly incomprehensible sights and experiences in a familiar, relatable way. The reader can put themselves in the world and imagine being there, because their perspective isn't so different from that of the character.

As for coming up with those sights and experiences, I've loved astronomy and space my entire life. I'm always researching, looking for wilder, more amazing creations I can bring to life, then throw characters into the middle of them.

What authors, past or present, got you jazzed about writing SF?

Goodness, I've been reading science fiction since I was a kid. In the old days, Isaac Asimov for the sweeping space exploration and fantastical future, Frank Herbert for the deep world- and culture-building. Later, Catherine Asaro for daring to mix serious, hard science fiction with romance and Lois McMaster Bujold for daring to have fun with science fiction. William Gibson for painting masterful imagery with mere words and Peter F. Hamilton for telling vast, grand stories.

RE/GENESIS

Re/Genesis

AN
Aurora
Rhapsody

AR

Short Story

G. S. Jennsen

In a future too distant to measure, a hyper-evolved breed of humans calling themselves Anadens rule multiple galaxies and alien species with an iron fist. But a small group of dissidents are willing to pursue any and all measures, no matter how extreme, to return freedom to the universe. Now one rebel Anaden will make the ultimate sacrifice in order to break the reigning Directorate's stranglehold on civilization—however many times it takes.

Set just prior to the events of *Relativity: Aurora Resonant Book One*, *RE/GENESIS* pulls back the veil on the universe of Amaranthe, where the fate of all living beings—human, alien and synthetic—will soon be decided.

*

Re/Genesis is unique in several respects. If you're current on the novels, then you know a major shift in setting, plot and tone occurs for the final trilogy, Aurora Resonant. *Set between* Abysm, *the last book in the* Aurora Renegades *trilogy and* Relativity, *the first book in Aurora Resonant, Re/Genesis provides a glimpse into this new world. It stars one of the most interesting, dynamic and confounding characters I've ever written—and one who became an instant fan favorite after* Relativity—*Eren asi-Idoni.*

Thanks to the radical change in scenery, Re/Genesis *works well as a self-contained story.*

DRAMATIS PERSONAE

Eren asi-Idoni

Anarch resistance agent.

Species: *Anaden*

Maeli

Anarch resistance agent.

Species: *Novoloume*

"The only way to deal with an unfree world is to become so absolutely free that your very existence is an act of rebellion."

— *Albert Camus*

AMARANTHE

PHOENIX ARX

MILKY WAY SECTOR 14

When you're an anarch, dying is the easy part. Completing your mission objective before nulling out? Not always so easy.

"A scan of your credentials does not return a valid result. Present Accepted credentials or be pacified."

The weaponized arm pointed at my chest by the Vigil unit suggested the pacification would not be of the gentle sort. It rarely was.

I brought my hands up from behind my back and stretched them into the air, fingers curled in but giving every indication they were opening in surrender. As the nail of my left index finger reached the center of my palm, I flicked it outward.

The gossamer dampener net unfurled as it sailed through the air to envelop the Vigil unit.

The floating orb began jerking to and fro in the narrow hallway in an attempt to unsnarl itself. I leapt forward and collected the edges of the net in one hand, then wrangled it under some semblance of control until I was able to wrap my arms around the wide, circular frame and brace it against the wall.

It squirmed savagely, but after two tries I found the input port and shoved a spike into it.

"Not this time, Vigil. You don't get me yet."

The unit dropped from my grip to the floor and rolled into the opposite wall.

I'd bought myself twenty minutes.

I stripped off my infiltration suit, shrank it and stuffed it in my kit. The fete-worthy attire which remained looked ridiculous to my mind, but nevertheless appropriate to the venue I'd be visiting. I unbound my hair and began scaling the service duct.

R

The galactic core hung in the sky like an ornament placed *just so* to best complement the pavilion. The prodigious light it provided, even here on the verge, filtered through an invisible prism field to cast soft, color-varying rays upon the conveniently reflective flooring.

See how small you are, it whispered.

See how powerful we are, it hummed.

In this case the core acted as a stand-in for the Anaden Directorate, obviously.

The guests enjoying the Phoenix Arx amenities acted oblivious to the implied message, though in truth it was because most of them had internalized it decades if not centuries ago and would never question it again.

Yet as a backup if the message didn't come through clearly enough—the Directorate didn't practice subtlety—every rotation of the Arx brought them a stunning view of the Phoenix Gateway in the distance. The colossal triple rings gleamed in the unfiltered glow of the galaxy, beautiful and menacing. This close to the ancient structure, the Gateway appeared more massive than the core itself. It was an optical illusion, but an effective one.

Today the Phoenix Gateway numbered only one of hundreds of its kind; in comparison to many of them it was aging, if not decrepit. But there was a reason for that: it was the *first*. The first wormhole portal to span the interstellar void and link to another galaxy. A dwarf galaxy, true, and one long since fallen out of fashion.

But once upon a time the Phoenix Gateway had meant *every-thing*. This meant it still mattered today, if only as a symbol of all the Directorate had achieved over the millennia.

I noted all this in passing, obscured behind a mask of jaded disdain as I traipsed across the pavilion in a manner which said 'standing in seemingly open space with the galactic core as a backdrop is so very passé. I'm bored already.' I made sure my eyes were vaguely unfocused, since as a member of the Idoni Dynasty I would be presumed by all in attendance to be high on at least one hypnol, more likely several. Always, lest the horror of existence come crashing in.

My assigned contact worked the delectables area of the pavilion that stretched the length of the left side. I wove my way through a sea of patrons, trying to balance the disinterested attitude against the reality that I was on a short timetable.

A virtual overlay in my vision gave me a reference, but I only dared access the overlay in short pulses. On an Arx an unauthorized comm network became perilously susceptible to detection, and detection was guaranteed to bring a merciless punishment.

The Novoloume who the overlay proclaimed was my contact meandered among the crowd dispensing dollops of hypnols onto the tongues and into the eyeballs of buzzing Anaden revelers with a smooth grace which was as mesmerizing as it was expected. Her shimmery pearl skin transformed the light from the core into rainbows, the hues shifting as she did.

I shook my head as minimally as possible in an effort to break out of the reverie before I approached her.

She held the dispenser aloft, ready to provide a dose of synthesized bliss. I started to decline when she placed an elongated, delicate hand on my waist with a sultry smile. Her breath wafted across my ear as she leaned in.

"I know, my dear, but one must maintain appearances. Trust me."

Trust was not something that came easily in my world. But this was *her* world… I offered the tip of my tongue while glaring a fierce warning at her.

The tip of the dispenser touched it, but no further sensation followed. It was empty.

First test passed. I nodded politely. "I'm Eren asi-Idoni."

"You may call me Maeli."

"But it's not your name."

She shrugged faintly as her gaze drifted over my shoulder. "It is as much a name as I allow myself to have. It is the same for you, no?"

"No. Eren asi-Idoni *is* my name."

"Yet the soul behind the name no longer exists, does it?"

I cut my eyes into the crowd, searching for threats. This was all getting far too mystical for my tastes. "Not in the Annals. I'm on a tight schedule here, so—"

"Dance with me." Her hands grasped mine in a display of surprising strength.

"I don't dance."

"All Idoni dance."

"Damn, that must be why I never fit in with them."

She pulled me closer. "There is a Praesidis Inquisitor approaching. *Dance with me.*"

I didn't panic, but I did allow her to sweep me along the smooth pavilion floor as I reviewed my limited options.

I kept a neural layer on tap which allowed me to pass as a proper Idoni connected to the integral on casual contact with other Idoni Dynasty members. But Praesidis members always saw through the charade. Praesidis Inquisitors, doubly so. And once they did, it was a swift trip to null for me.

The fact I wasn't already dead, however, meant the Inquisitor hadn't come here for me. If I played the part of a... well, a typical Idoni, I stood a chance of escaping notice.

I tried to relax in her embrace and flow with her movements. She was of course correct about the dancing—the natural, innate rhythm was encoded in my genetics. Annoyed, I allowed instinct to take over.

"You have stunning eyes. They are as twin starbursts in the night sky."

I swallowed, feeling heady enough I started to wonder how empty the dispenser had been. "Stop doing that."

"Doing what?" She swept me between two other dancers in a lengthy, dramatic spin.

"That thing you're doing."

"It is not a thing I am doing, Eren asi-Idoni. It is a thing I *am*."

So all the Novoloume insisted. The pheromones they secreted were not *intended* to send most mammalian species into a sexual froth; in fact, they had no knowledge of such an effect until they encountered those species.

I'd insist as strongly it was a lie they professed to hide the nature of their blatant manipulation of others, except the talent hadn't gained them any greater freedom than the other species were permitted. Still, it was no wonder they had been decreed an Accepted Species in record time following contact. Rumor had it the Idoni Primor kept a stable of twenty Novoloume as pets.

I wasn't immune to her beauty, both real and sense-induced— the Novoloume, regardless of gender, were among the most lovely sapient creatures living. I was nonetheless able to resist the mesmeric aspects of her presence, but the act of resisting was itself distracting. I tried to focus my thoughts on other, more relevant matters.

"Is the Inquisitor gone yet?"

She smiled blithely. The core spun around us, or us around the core. "Nearly. He is currently disposing of a troublesome Ch'mshak."

That sounded like a show worthy of observing, but I didn't dare cast my gaze toward it. "Successfully?"

"If bloodily." Her attention flitted to the left then back to me, and her tone remained studiously casual. "You are the first Anaden anarch I've worked with."

"There aren't so many of us. It's not an easy task, breaking away from the integral."

"I can imagine."

"You really can't."

Her chin dipped. "As you say. The Inquisitor has departed the pavilion."

"Good." I grasped one of her hands firmly and dropped the other. "I'm in a bit of a rush. I was told you could get me into the maintenance channel, so make that happen."

"As you wish." Her manner became purposeful but no less graceful as she guided me past the crowd to the staff area and onward to the rear wall. A server unit dawdled above a cylindrical tunnel, and Maeli indicated for me to wait.

When it vacated, she gestured to the tunnel. I peered down it to get an idea of what awaited us.

It was tailored for product delivery, not personal travel, and it held no transport implement.

I raised a questioning eyebrow at my escort. "You know how to do this?"

She nodded.

"Then, after you." No way was I plunging into the unknown shadowy depths and leaving her standing up here surrounded by every creature comfort, where she might decide the trip wasn't worth taking.

A flash of defiance sparked in her magenta irises as she leapt into the shaft. *3... 2... 1...* and I followed.

Falling.

The towering Arx had a thousand levels. I suspected I'd be doing so for a while. The snug, curving walls whooshed by in silence, unmarked and unrelenting. They threatened to become as suffocating as the Idoni integral had been.

I closed my eyes and concentrated on the mission details.

The ways in which the mission could fail were legion.

A thruster suit was impossible to smuggle onto the Arx. A stealth, external breach by vessel ipso facto failed due to strict security protocols. An antimatter-tipped long-range missile, in the improbable event it penetrated said security, stood to cause significant damage, but not enough. Multiple distributed detonations were required, and follow-up missiles would doubtless be intercepted.

Turning a ship into an antimatter bomb was arguably viable in theory but an absurd risk in practice. The amount of antimatter needed to be stored on the ship in order for the reaction to reach the target when the vessel ignited was so large it created a sixty-eight percent chance of blowing early.

The solution—or the best solution my superiors had concocted—was a solitary incursion via the channel the maintenance and repair drones used to access the structure. It stretched the three megameters from the Arx in a series of magnetized coils which propelled objects traveling within them forward through space.

It wasn't as fast as a thruster suit, but I would ride the stream to its destination, just like the drones did.

I chuckled quietly, though the analogy to the Anaden drones above, to when I'd been little more than a drone myself, was too evident to bother enunciating.

The increased resistance against the soles of my feet manifested a bare second before my descent slowed to an abrupt halt. The braking mechanism was designed for less squishy objects than organic limbs.

I landed on the floor with a jarring thud… and found Maeli waiting on me stoically, the swirls of her lustrous robe unruffled and in their befitting place.

It ought not to come as a surprise to me that this, too, was a skill the Novoloume had perfected.

Well, *one* of us no longer felt obliged to project an expected appearance for onlookers. I gathered the copper cords of my hair up off my back and secured them, then ditched the majority of the dress attire. Best to wait to don the hazard suit until we reached the channel.

She motioned me forward. "The passageways proceed for some distance. If your time is as limited as you say, we should make haste."

In my life I had an eternity's worth of time—and right now, none at all, so I adopted the haste.

This deep in the bowels of the Arx, everything was mechanized. Not an organic in sight. Better yet, not a Vigil unit in sight, either, for the Directorate had no need to police their shackled and neutered machines.

Let the citizens dance the night away above, secure in their warped caricature of a free existence. Let the machines do the work. Peace and harmony reigns…

…but not unchallenged. Not tonight.

After crossing an expansive assembly floor we took a left down a short, wide corridor ending in a force field. Maeli stopped.

"The maintenance channel begins on the other side."

"Understood." I put my kit on the floor, opened it and retrieved the hazard suit, then began tugging the snug material on.

Once it covered my waist, I eyed her grimly. "The Arx should be far enough away to survive the blast, but if you've got a new locale in mind, it wouldn't hurt to head in that direction close to now."

"I seldom linger in any one location. It will take me a few moments to reach the transport wing and depart, but no longer than it will take you to reach your target." She paused, looking uneasy. "I'm confident in my ability to achieve shelter, but how will you reach a safe distance before the detonation?"

Suit in place, I re-secured the utility belt on my hips. "I won't."

The silence hung a span too long. "Oh." Another gap of silence. "Is it painful?"

I snapped both ends of the explosives ribbon to the belt. Carefully. "Almost always."

"Then your sacrifices for the cause are even greater than I realized."

"No need to make a scene over it." *Sacrifice* was such an empty word, tossed about by those who weren't engaging in it to make themselves feel better. I did not and would never know Maeli well enough to say if this was her purpose in using it. Didn't really matter either way.

Satisfied the ribbon was secure and not exploding, I gazed up at her. "What else do you have for me?"

"I'm sending you the drones' ID frequency. Broadcast it, and they'll take you for one of their own—unless you bump into one. So... don't."

"Noted. No dancing with the drones."

"Since you don't dance, I trust that will not be a problem."

I laughed for her. These flares of irreverence were probably a clue pointing to why she acted as an anarch. Part of me toyed with wishing I'd get the opportunity to find out more about her reasons... until I remembered I didn't do attachments.

I situated the breather skin over my face and reattached the depleted kit to the belt as well. "Time to do this. Thank you for your help, Maeli. *Nos libertatem somnia.*"

"*Nos libertatem somnia,* Eren asi-Idoni."

I slowed my respiration rhythm to maximize the effectiveness of the breather skin. Then I stepped through the force field separating the corridor from the entry tube.

Three rapid steps to the exit and I pitched into space toward the Phoenix Gateway.

The channel coils would get me to my destination eventually, but I pulled my arms in and mimicked a missile to help the propulsion system along.

The journey was much like the fall down the service tunnel, excepting the scenery. My deliberate revolutions presented me with views of the Arx, the Gateway, the galactic core and the intergalactic void in turn.

The once imposing Arx profile quickly shrank in the shadow of the mammoth Gateway. Each ring measured a kilometer thick and a hundred meters wide; the rig driving them weighed greater than six teratonnes. It had been built to last, and no conventional weapon an anarch might procure was capable of destroying it.

But even the strongest creations could not withstand the application of a fundamental law of physics. Matter and antimatter could not exist in the same space, and their collision was going to result in the expulsion of energy on the order of eight hundred peta-joules—and perhaps most importantly, the annihilation of the matter/antimatter which triggered it.

Presto, no more Gateway.

The first of the three rings grew large on my horizon as the terminus of the channel neared. Right before I reached it I brought my legs up to hit the outer boundary at full speed, sprint across its breadth and launch off the structure in free flight toward the center loop.

The Gateway activated, heralding an incoming vessel from its twin in the Phoenix dwarf galaxy. The pulsing energy slammed into me, sending me spinning off course. I skidded out of control over the rim of the ring and grasped the edge with fingertips to spare.

Of all the cursed timing.

I adjusted my grip, trying my damnedest not to pant. Oxygen was a mite scarce resource in space, and now that I was out here I had what I had and no more.

"Well, hell." Nobody was apt to notice an Anaden dangling off the side of one of the loops, legs swaying about in open space, right? Maybe I should stay here for a while....

But there existed no room for such luxuries in my life. The morbid irony implied in the notion I considered the act a luxury didn't escape my notice as I hauled myself up over the ledge and stood on the flat surface of the ring to survey matters.

From here, the void to my right loomed as darkly shrouded as the core to my left shone bright. It felt as if I stood on the precipice of not merely a galaxy but existence itself. It was indulgent of me. Also dizzying, but dizzy was not something I needed to be at the moment.

I removed the ribbon of explosive slabs from my belt, careful to orient it in the correct direction so I would place them in the desired order. The protective layer was set to start dissolving as soon as it came into contact with the metal comprising the exterior; therefore I had to start with the slab bearing the thickest layer in order to buy time to position them all.

I detached the first slab from the ribbon, stuck it to the metal at my feet—and ran. Five kilometers to the next target location, and the reaper's clock counting down on me like a shadow nipping at my heels.

The balls of my feet barely hit the surface as I soared from stride to stride. Lacking oxygen, my muscles used my body's stored energy reserves to fuel my movements. The minimal gravitational effect the power rig generated for the drones kept me from flying off into space, while also allowing me to travel at greatly enhanced speed.

A virtual bullseye marked the next site. The ideal placement and spacing had been worked out in advance by anarch scientists, or engineers, or whoever it was who sat in labs and did those things so people like me could venture outside and… *complete the missions.*

I hardly stopped as I released the slab, not wanting to lose any momentum.

When the clock hit zero I would be dead, but right now I was alive. High on oxygen deprivation, the magnificent view, and the act of running free along the curving arc of an apparatus that warped the fabric of spacetime to sling objects and people 430 kiloparsecs in a frozen, boundless instant. The stars at my back, the universe at my fingertips—

—a drone clambered up the lip of the ring just as my foot hit metal. I tripped hard over it, landed on my ass with a painful *crack* and tumbled across the surface.

The drone landed on top of me before I could move. One of its spindly tool arms sliced through my shoulder as the other poked for my face.

With a groan I kicked at it and skittered away to climb to my feet. Undeterred, the drone sprang toward me.

"Off you go, machine!" I grabbed it with both hands and hurled it over the side into oblivion.

The cut on my shoulder hurt like a bitch, but worse, the swipe had sliced open the thin film of my suit. My dwindling life expectancy had now been cut in half.

But it hadn't damaged my legs, so I ran once again. Two primed slabs still to place.

If I failed, the destruction might not be total. This constituted an unacceptable outcome. To my superiors, but mostly to me. I did not do half-measures, and if I was going to die in an explosion of white hot agony, it was going to be a properly majestic explosion.

One which served as a fitting symbol of how far we were willing to go to dismantle the Directorate superstructure and break its chokehold on not solely us but the entire fucking universe.

The near vacuum of space sucked at the tear in my suit, but I ignored it to sprint. Only a little farther.

That was such a lie.

The light of the core sank above me as the ring bowed in to the void. The marker for the next-to-last location blinked urgently at me, and I readied the drop—

—and very nearly made a disaster of it. The tiny sips of oxygen I subsisted on were taking their toll, and when coupled with the pain in my arm and leaking suit, I was now less running and more stumbling forward from sheer inertia.

I tried to drop the slab while moving, slipped and kicked it toward the edge. I lunged for it in panic, overestimated the distance, and fell atop it. *Please don't detonate. Please don't detonate.*

One thing was certain: my weight had succeeded in sticking it to the metal. I crawled to my feet and rested my hands on my thighs. Dizziness—the real kind—blurred the periphery of my vision.

"Why am I doing this?"

The stars had no answer for me, but it was okay. I had my own answer. I would run and I would fly and I would die, but I would not be a slave. Not to the Idoni integral and its sadistic Primor. Not to the Anaden Directorate. Not to my anarch superiors. I wasn't here because they'd ordered me here; I was here to be free.

I ran.

Possibly crookedly.

The journey passed in a blur, and suddenly the final location rushed up on me.

I placed the slab, knowing it had none but the slimmest protective layer, and flung myself off the ring into space.

Time's up.

I twisted around to face the Gateway with a second to spare. A second to witness the staccato of explosions shine more brilliantly than the galactic core as my body atomized to nothingness, until not even stardust remained.

ANARCH POST ALPHA

MILKY WAY SECTOR 59

On the other side of the galaxy, deep in a sector the Directorate had long ago abandoned, I awoke with a gasp.

Sterile smooth walls and cushioned linens welcomed my transition. A fading echo of the flash of agony receded to a memory as I breathed in the oxygen-rich air of the restoration capsule.

My hand went to my shoulder, but of course the wound was gone. My skin felt cool, still moist from the gelatinous fluid it had resided in until needed.

Outside the capsule a Curative unit checked my vitals. A chime signaled all systems were nominal, and the protective cover slid away as the virtual image of my handler materialized.

"Welcome back, Eren. Congratulations on a successful mission. See to your personals, then report in twenty minutes for a briefing on your next assignment. *Nos libertatem somnia.*"

Q&A FOR *RE/GENESIS*
INCLUDED IN
BEYOND THE STARS: AT GALAXY'S EDGE

Re/Genesis features a fantastical, far-future world very different from our own. Where did the story come from, and how does it relate to your other works?

This is the first time I've ventured into far-future territory in my writing, but it won't be the last. When I wrote the story, I was just starting work on the final trilogy in my *Aurora Rhapsody* series, *Aurora Resonant*, which is going to take place almost entirely in the world of *Re/Genesis*. The main characters in *Aurora Rhapsody* have known for several books now that another universe—the 'true' universe, as it were—exists alongside our own, but *Re/Genesis* is the first real look anyone's gotten at it.

This story started out as a sort of test run, a chance for me to dip my toe into the waters of the worldbuilding I was going to have to do for the next trilogy. But I quickly fell in love with the character of Eren and completely embraced the story, setting and all. It got me legitimately excited to dive into writing *Aurora Resonant*.

Who are your favorite fictional heroes and villains?

I'm an avid video gamer (though I have little time to play since I began writing full time), so I'd have to say my favourite fictional hero is Commander Shepard from the Mass Effect video game trilogy. Favourite villain? Probably the motiles from Peter F. Hamilton's Pandora Star/Judas Unchained space opera novels. He wrote a number of chapters from their perspective, and their way of thinking, their worldview, their entire essence was so foreign and, well, alien. It was fascinating.

MERIDIAN

MERIDIAN

AN AURORA RHAPSODY

SHORT STORY

G. S. JENNSEN

When terrorists carpet-bomb an Earth Alliance colony, killing thousands, the military must bring the perpetrators to justice.

Strangers thrown together by circumstance amidst a difficult mission, nobody expects Lieutenants David Solovy and Richard Navick to be heroes. In fact, their commanding officers would prefer they stay out of the way and out of trouble. But when the mission to bring the One World Separatists terrorist group to justice goes sideways, they must take matters into their own hands if they want to save the day, get the bad guys and live to tell the tale.

Set nearly half a century before *STARSHINE: Aurora Rising Book One (Amaranthe #1)*, *Meridian* is the unlikely story of how one of the greatest friendships of *Aurora Rhapsody* came to be.

*

The newest story and an exclusive to this Collection, Meridian *reveals how David Solovy and Richard Navick first met. This is an encounter I've wanted to recount for a long time—and one readers have asked for repeatedly—but due to larger plot considerations, it needed to wait until now to be shared.*

This story is best read between Rubicon *and* Requiem, *but so long as you've read the first couple of books (enough to feel like you know Richard and, through flashbacks, David), you should get full enjoyment out of it.*

DRAMATIS PERSONAE

Lieutenant David Solovy
Marine Special Operations, EA SE Regional Command.
Faction: *Earth Alliance*

Lieutenant Richard Navick
EA Military Intelligence.
Faction: *Earth Alliance*

Commander Frederik Becker
Marine Special Operations, EA SE Regional Command.
Faction: *Earth Alliance*

Captain Antonio Cassano
Marine Special Operations, EA SE Regional Command.
Faction: *Earth Alliance*

Second Lieutenant Troy Mendoza
Marine Special Operations, EA SE Regional Command.
Faction: *Earth Alliance*

Captain Eleni Gianno
Marine Special Operations, EA NE Regional Command.
Faction: *Earth Alliance*

Gannor Tai
Leader, One World Separatists.
Faction: *Independent*

"The meeting of two personalities is like the contact of two chemical substances: if there is any reaction, both are transformed."

— Carl Jung

2280

(42 YEARS BEFORE THE EVENTS OF STARSHINE)

AFS BRISBANE

C louds the color of molded moss roiled across the sky like thunderheads of a squall line, yet driven by some unnatural force. Scattered glimpses of the surface soon disappeared beneath the churning storm as it devoured the horizon.

Lieutenant David Solovy was hurrying through the breakroom when the dramatic scene caught his attention. He stopped in the middle of the room to stare at the news feed.

"These visuals are coming in to us from satellites orbiting New Marrakesh following a series of explosions in the skies above the colony's largest settlement. They are minutes old, and the situation appears to still be in flux. We've thus far been unable to establish reliable communications with officials on the ground."

New Marrakesh was a third wave colony, founded a decade earlier. Small, but growing fast. Quirky, in honor of its namesake—or so he had heard.

Someone jostled David's shoulder, and he glanced over to see the room filling up with Marines eager to crowd in around the wall screens. The scattered murmurs were uncharacteristically hushed, however; no one wanted to drown out the reporters.

"We've received a communication relating to the events on New Marrakesh. It purports to originate from the One World Separatists terrorist group."

Not them again. The bombastic group of thugs bearing the head-scratching title had been flooding exanet interest spheres with propaganda for weeks now. Their screeds quoted everyone from Plato to Mao Tse-Tung to rationalize their philosophy of...well, no one was really sure, other than it included an irrational hatred of the Earth Alliance government.

"The communication states the following:

> *'The Earth Alliance was warned. You were all warned. The universe belongs to all and none, and it will not be debased by the filthy, clamoring hands of Alliance usurpers. Their contamination must be cleansed from the universe. It tried to spread to the formerly pure world you call New Marrakesh, but it will spread no farther. New Marrakesh is being cleansed, but it is only the first. The line is drawn here, today. World by world, we will reclaim the universe in the name of all and none.'"*

"Bloody psychos." Troy Mendoza, a Second Lieutenant in David's regiment, gestured dismissively in the direction of the screens. "Point me to their hole in the ground, and I'll show them what cleansing looks like."

David muttered a vague commiseration, if only to shut the kid up. His zeal was commendable, but he was young and hadn't earned his boasting.

David's brow furrowed in growing concern as he took in the continuous stream of worsening visuals. What had the terrorists unleashed?

The death toll on New Marrakesh had surpassed 64,000 when military intelligence located the One World Separatists headquarters. No more than 109,000 people were *on* New Marrakesh the day of the attack, so the trend didn't bode well for the balance.

Eighty aerial dispersal bombs had detonated an insidious, homebrewed chemical-radioactive mixture in the lower atmosphere of the planet, where New Marrakesh's notoriously turbulent weather patterns were primed to pick it up, thus increasing the poison's destructiveness while expanding its reach. Concentrated chlorine gas was ignited by miniature nuclear bombs to quickly become hydrochloric acid in the clouds then fall as radioactive rain to the surface. The chlorine that didn't transform immediately sank to the surface to choke everyone in a ten-kilometer radius. Meanwhile, the volatile compounds saturated the clouds, transforming into a variety of deadly substances and spreading across the landscape. Standard dilution measures might sterilize the air eventually, but not before they made things worse.

Whatever the worth of OWS' cause—and whatever OWS' cause *was*—it could never justify indiscriminate killing of civilians. The people trying to make a go of it on New Marrakesh didn't deserve to die, and they absolutely didn't deserve to die in some of the most horrific ways imaginable.

So on hearing a strike against the terrorists' headquarters was in the works, David reported to the briefing room of the *EAS Brisbane* displaying a level of enthusiasm he hadn't felt of late. Not since the confrontation with Becker last month, anyway.

He snagged a seat next to the captain of his squad, Antonio Cassano. "What's the word, Captain?"

Cassano smirked. "Word is, we've got them."

Commander Becker cleared his throat loudly from the front of the room. "Marines, pay attention. EAMI agents have located a compound on Radavi believed to be the headquarters for the One World Separatists. Reconnaissance has captured the following visuals of the site."

The screen behind Becker displayed a cluster of warehouse-style buildings on the outskirts of a town.

"This central building is thought to be the command center. The structures surrounding it house supplies, bunks and ancillary supplies. *This* building—Becker indicated the largest structure, located off to the side from the main cluster—is a chemical factory. It is operational."

Someone in the back of the room leapt to their feet. "They're planning to hit other colonies?"

"Sit down, Cadet. Evidence suggests they are, yes. The suspected leader of OWS, Gannor Tai, arrived at the compound this morning. Most of his senior advisors are also in residence today, putting a total of thirty-one individuals on site. We will arrive at Radavi in two hours. An aerial strike is apt to ignite the volatile chemicals present in the factory and put the nearby civilian settlement at risk.

"Therefore, our mission is to infiltrate the compound, secure the factory and kill-or-capture Gannor Tai as well as all other persons present on the compound." Becker entered a command on his control panel. "Your assignments are out to you now. Meet in the designated rooms for squad briefings in ten minutes. We are boots on the ground in two and half hours."

David opened the incoming assignment file in eVi, scanned it and groaned. If Becker wanted to keep punishing him with crap assignments until this rotation ended, there wasn't a blasted thing he could do about it. But sidelining him on a mission where success truly mattered? If people died while David was left twiddling his thumbs, words would be exchanged...inevitably followed by another reprimand. Possibly a suspension. Damn it.

ᴙ

RADAVI

EARTH ALLIANCE COLONY
SOUTHEAST QUADRANT OF SETTLED SPACE

Dry wind swept dust across David's skin in waves of scorching pinpricks. The promotional brochures insisted Radavi wasn't a desert, merely 'arid.' Two minutes on the ground, he was of the firm opinion that the sales pitch was *chush' sobach'ya*.

A blinking green dot on one of his two whisper virtual screens marked the location of his contact from military intelligence. His eyes sought and found the location on the terrain: seventy meters ahead to the northwest, in a gully rimmed by plants that were definitely *not* cacti. Because if they were cacti, this would be a desert.

In the valley to his left, the OWS compound bustled with furtive activity amid the encroaching shadows of dusk. The functionality of his cloaking shield didn't merit the term 'invisibility,' but when tuned to the—wait for it—*desert* setting, he was confident it kept him from being from seen from the valley or picked up by sensors.

He moved carefully through the scrub grass toward the marked location. When he was ten meters out, he sent his contact a heads-up of his imminent arrival so nobody got shot or stabbed. A few seconds later, he dropped to his stomach and shimmied in beside the man, who lay prone on the high point of the steppe. He offered a hand. "Lieutenant David Solovy."

The man studied one of three tiny holos arrayed in an arc in front of him while he absently extended a hand out to David. "Lieutenant Richard Navick. Since I do what I'm told, I didn't question my CO, but now that you're here, I will question you. Why are you here?"

David gave him a closed-mouth smile. "To acquire the latest intel on the situation at this compound here and relay it to my superiors prior to them moving in."

Navick shook his head. "I can relay the information to anyone who needs it. I *have* been relaying it to my CO all day. Do they not trust my reports?"

"I'm confident they do. It's not you, it's me."

Navick grimaced. "Is this a recon run or a break-up?"

David stifled a laugh on account of subterfuge. "The former, I hope. No, the assignment is Commander Becker's way of punishing me today for a tiny insubordination incident last month—to be distinguished from his ways of punishing yesterday and the day before. Basically, I'm fucked for the remainder of my rotation. Alas, but let's get this done. Tell me, Lieutenant, what do you see?"

"A hornet's nest of complications for our people." He flicked one of the holos, and the image shifted. "The biggest problem is that the chemical factory is rigged with explosives, and, though I haven't been able to put eyes on it, I suspect Gannor Tai is carrying the trigger in his pocket."

"That *is* a problem."

"Yes. We've also got four guards outside the factory, eight patrolling the compound perimeter and six on the command center, all armed with TSGs sporting black market mods. Everyone inside is armed, but only with Daemons, which is...better. The building on the far southwest is the armory, so it will need to be blocked off first thing. Tai's office is two-thirds of the way through the command center. Our people can expect a gauntlet of close combat to reach him."

"Fabulous. Well, let me put my extensive special forces training and experience to use and pass the information along to Becker."

He did exactly that, then watched the resulting orders roll out to the infiltration squads on his second whisper screen.

"Can you pipe the feed from the cam you've got tailing Tai into the mission channel? A stealthed drone is going to drop targeted munitions directly above his office or, alternatively, wherever he happens to be when the infiltration squads are ready to move in."

Navick punched in a few commands on the panel lying in front of him. "Done. I hope the drone is precise and the munitions powerful."

"You and me both. Chemical burns are not on my social calendar for this week."

Silence fell for a moment, so David motioned to the holos. "Are all those coming from bot cams?"

Navick nodded, reaching to his right and retrieving something from his pack. He opened his palm to reveal an orb four centimeters in diameter. He tapped on it, and it vanished behind a faint shimmer, no more noticeable than a heat shimmer, even from less than a meter away.

"Nice."

"They are handy. They can be actively controlled, set to a pattern or tagged to a marker, including particular thermal signatures—bodies, usually. An internal power source keeps them running for up to three weeks at a time with constant video and audio transmission. I've got four of them roaming the grounds, one inside the factory and two inside the command center."

"Smooth work." David glanced around, tweaking the near infrared filter on his ocular implant to compensate for the deepening shadows as night descended. "And you've been lying here watching their feeds for...what? Ten hours?"

Navick cracked his neck and massaged a shoulder. "Try eighteen."

"Damn. I hesitate to ask, but if they transmit their feeds to remote receivers, can't they transmit them somewhere else? Why are *you* here?"

"Official guidelines about HumInt backing up automated intel whenever possible. And to be fair, I've had to modify their parameters a couple of times based on activity in the compound. Yes, it's grunt work, but it's probably necessary grunt work."

"As opposed to my grunt work."

Navick tilted his head in concession.

Chattered erupted on the mission channel, and David perked up, his gaze instinctively scanning the horizon. "The infiltration squads are moving in. Can you get a cam on the northwest perimeter?"

"I can do better." Navick produced a scope and zoomed it in to the northwest.

David scooted closer to be able to see the scope's screen. When their shoulders touched, he peered over at Navick. "You're not going to try to kiss me, are you?"

"Nope. You are not my type."

David frowned. It had been quite subtle, but the lieutenant had cased him on his arrival, and not for potential threats. "Are you sure?"

"I am."

"But—"

"You're far too gregarious, and I suspect inherently arrogant. Also Russian—I mean, how have you not lost that accent yet? Give you a little time, and you'll doubtless turn out to be a showboater, too."

David frowned. "I won't dispute the criticisms, but what you don't know is that I'm also a fantastic cook—my mother taught me everything her mother knew. And I've been told on multiple occasions that I have seductive eyes."

"Oh, dear Lord. You can stop now."

"I also—"

"Please don't tell me your 'also.'"

David worked to keep a straight face. "Fine...consider me put in my place."

"Good, because the fireworks are about to start."

Instantly on alert, he watched the scope screen as a dozen figures advanced toward the south façade of the command center from the west. They neared to twenty meters—

"Tai's on the move."

—an explosion rocked the east third of the building. Flames and debris exploded outward, then collapsed in a concave arc as the roof crumbled. The Marines fanned out and rushed forward to infiltrate the structure.

Navick tracked movement on one of the holos, zooming in as close as the visual allowed. A figure moved slowly, possibly limping, down a hallway into a larger room. "The strike missed Tai, at least partially."

"Shit." David accessed the mission channel. *"Commander, Target One is still active. I repeat, Target One is still active and on the move."*

Commander Becker (mission): "Copy that. Drone is tracking and—"

Laser fire erupted on the south side of the command center from both directions.

Captain Cassano (mission): "Turret fire on the perimeter! Take cover!"

Cadet Rove (mission): "I'm hit!"

Commander Becker (mission): "Retasking drone to disable turrets."

Screams filled the gaps in weapons fire to permeate the air. "Christ, they're getting torn apart! Where the hell did the turrets come from?"

Navick frantically adjusted cam angles. "It looks as if...they must have been buried underground. Shielded by dampeners so we wouldn't detect them."

Smaller explosions plumed as the drone fired on the turrets. On the mission comm, calls for help overlapped one another.

"We have to help them." David unlatched his Daemon and engaged the augmented barrel extension, braced on his elbows and sighted down in search of a target—

Navick's hand landed on his arm. "You'll alert them to our location."

"Not in this chaos." But he hesitated. Did it matter if the enemy knew where they were? They had the height advantage and could pick off advancing attackers without difficulty.

Unless they were going to do something crazy to salvage the operation.

He laid the weapon down and studied the scene. The crisscrossing fire died off as the drone succeeded in taking out the active turrets and adopted a defensive posture facing the command center. Protecting the Marines. Several guards rushed outward to continue the counter-attack, then were driven inside when the drone opened fire on them.

Captain Cassano (mission): "We've got four people down and five injured. We've retreated to defensible positions, but I don't know how long they'll stay that way. Orders, Commander?"

Commander Becker (mission): "We can't let this opportunity to take out OWS slip away. Hold for reinforcements."

From the *Brisbane*? It would take twenty minutes at a minimum for a new squad to reach the compound, during which time Tai's people could maneuver around the drone's envelope and start picking off the pinned-down Marines. Plus, if they had hidden turrets, what else did they have?

David breathed out through his nose. "Tai still on the grid?"

"Him and three of his people are moving around the interior. I assume he deduced he was being tracked and is trying to make that harder."

"All right. The fact he didn't blow the chemical factory when the attack began means he doesn't *want* to blow the chemical factory. He thinks he can survive this, escape and even salvage some materials before the cavalry arrives to obliterate this place. I see one of three scenarios playing out here.

"One, the reinforcements from the *Brisbane* get inside and corner Tai, and he blows the factory when they breach his bunker of choice. Two, OWS takes out our people on the ground before the reinforcements arrive, then a new firefight erupts throughout the compound when they do arrive. If our people win, we're back to the first scenario. Three, Tai and his people escape before the reinforcements arrive."

"None of those scenarios have us winning."

"They do not, which is why we need to make a fourth scenario happen. To start, we need to disable the remote detonation connection to the explosives rigged in the factory."

Navick didn't respond, and after a few seconds David looked over, eyebrow raised. "Well?"

"I'm thinking."

"Think faster."

Navick shot him a glare, but it faded as his lips pursed. "You'd need to get inside the factory. If I can see the circuit flow, I can tell you how to disable the signal receiver."

David contemplated the large building down the hill. "I've got stealth, but we'll need to distract the guards out front briefly. Assume for now we can make that happen. What do I do once I'm inside?"

ℛ

David crept toward the chemical factory, shrouded in a cloaking shield cranked up to full. Distant sounds marked the standoff on the other side of the command center, but here there was only eerie silence.

Richard: *"Your CO give you the go-ahead for this?"*

David: *"I didn't exactly clear it through Becker. If I told him the plan, he'd order me to stay put and wait for the reinforcements. But the way I see it, I can't disobey orders if I don't have any."*

Richard: *"It's your career."*

David: *"So far. Here goes."* Fifteen meters from the factory entrance, he palmed one of the grenades he'd brought. Cocked his arm back and let it sail.

It landed well past the two guards posted at the entrance and bounced off the façade of a nearby building. The next instant it detonated, tearing through the walls and igniting whatever was stored in it.

The guards jumped, then almost fucked the whole thing up by being unable to decide whether they should run toward the explosion or away from it. They finally opted for a third tactic, running parallel to the explosion like they intended to root out the perpetrators.

David sprinted lightly for the entrance and slipped inside, holding the door open an extra second to make certain the cloaked cam bot accompanying him made it in as well. The locations of the four explosive packages were marked on his whisper, and he skulked along the right interior wall until he reached the first one. In a minor boon, no human laborers worked on the lines, though the lines *were* running.

Just below eye level he found a bulky, rectangular module mounted on the wall. A smaller module was attached to it. *"I'm at the first explosive."*

Richard: "Slice the cover off the smaller module, no more than a centimeter deep."

David unsheathed his kinetic blade and activated it, slicing into the metal as fast as he dared. The front cover fell into his waiting hand, and he stuck it in a pocket of his tactical vest. *"What now?"*

Richard: "One second...see the square bundle at the junction of three fiber lines? Stab it."

David: "...stab it?"

Richard: "Yes. With the tip of your blade. Skewer it."

David's face screwed up. *"You got it."* He positioned the tip of his blade in front of the bundle of circuitry and jabbed it forward. He waited, but he didn't get so much as a sizzle. *"Nothing happened."*

Richard: "Yes, it did. Get to the next explosive and do the same thing to it."

David moved swiftly once he knew what he was searching for and what to do with it, and in less than two minutes he'd *skewered* the final explosives package. *"Done. What's the guards' status?"*

Richard: "Turning back your way now. Hurry and you can make it out before they come in sight of the door."

David sprinted for the entry and outside, taking a hard left toward Navick's perch on the hill above. *"I owe you a beer, Lieutenant. As soon as I get to a safe distance, I'll inform Becker the drone can pepper the command center at its leisure without worrying about Tai blowing—"*

A massive explosion lit the sky to daylight, and he rushed for the retreating shadows. *"The hell was that?"*

Commander Becker (mission): "Report!"

Captain Cassano (mission): "SAL on the roof took out the drone!"

David's shoulders sagged. Well, shit.

David: "Drone's down. Time for a new plan."

Richard: "Now that Tai can't set off the explosives, maybe you ought to wait on the reinforcements."

David: "Negative. Now they can fan out and search for the holed-up Marines. They've got a SAL on the roof, which means they can take out our people en masse when they find them. Get a cam bot on the roof, please."

Lieutenant Solovy (mission): "Alpha and Bravo Squads, you need to find new cover right now, and find it quietly. I'm coming to you, so kindly don't shoot me."

Commander Becker (mission): "Solovy, return to your post."

David sighed. So much for not disobeying orders….

Lieutenant Solovy (mission): "Commander, Lieutenant Navick will relay intel on the rooftop SAL activity to you and Alpha and Bravo Squads. Mendoza, if you can use the cam feed to target the SAL's wielder and get a shot, do it."

Becker continued to bark protests at him and instructions at the others, but David tuned them out to concentrate on avoiding detection as he crossed the breadth of the compound toward the scene of the initial ambush.

Cassano relayed the squads' new location to him on the sly, and he slipped past the rear façade of one of the ancillary buildings to reach them.

What was left of them, anyway. Near as he could tell, only two Marines were free of serious injury, and they did not include his captain.

He crouched beside Cassano. "You guys are a sorry lot."

Cassano had a death grip on a medwrap held over a thigh wound. "Yeah, yeah, we got our asses kicked. What's your excuse?"

"I was working on my tan. Did the remote detonation bombs make it here?"

Cassano winced and tilted his head in the direction of one of the other Marines propped against the exterior wall. "Gianno's got them. What are you planning?"

"To finish the mission. Hang in there." He clapped his captain's shoulder and moved to where Cassano had gestured.

Captain Eleni Gianno and three members of her unit had joined the *Brisbane* a week earlier to bulk up the Marine tactical detachment, and he'd never worked with her. But there were no strangers in a foxhole, as it were, so he skipped the introductions to kneel beside her.

A full roll's worth of medwraps wound around her upper arm, shoulder and across her neck; he didn't want to guess at the extent of her injuries.

"I need your bombs and the trigger signal."

She nudged the pack beside her over to him. "Coverage is twenty-eight square meters per. There are eight in the pack, more than enough for the whole building. Stick them, toss them, it doesn't matter. They're fairly stable, so don't throw them in a fire or one of the chemical vats and they won't detonate prematurely. The trigger signal is FK41B on a 52 MHz wave."

"Understood. Thanks."

She jerked a sharp nod despite her injuries, and he stood and slung the pack on his back.

"Take us with you."

He pivoted to Mendoza, who stood next to one of Gianno's men. "You have grenades?"

"Four of them."

David reached in his pack and retrieved a grenade. "Now you have five. Mendoza, get on your rifle and take out that SAL on the roof. When the terrorists come for this location, light them up with grenades. I'm counting on you to protect your injured squadmates."

Mendoza frowned, then straightened up and saluted. "Yes, sir!"

Behind him, Cassano grumbled under his breath. "The commander is yelling at me to stop you from doing something stupid. I explained to him that the restraints we brought for the terrorists were lying in tatters forty meters away next to Ovale's body, and since I couldn't walk I lacked the ability to physically keep you here. Don't make me regret it."

"No promises, Captain." David reactivated his cloaking shield and headed for the command center.

⋊R

David: "Navick, you've got to be my eyes now. You and the cam bot. I've named him Yevgeni."

Richard: "You can tell me why over that beer."

David: "Sounds good."

He palmed his now sole grenade and studied the main entrance, where three guards paced in agitation and whispered to one another in hushed shouts. He figured they were trying to decide if they should go in search of the Marines so the SAL could take them out, but were worried what the infiltrators might have up their sleeves.

He readied himself and lobbed the grenade at the front door.

Bodies went flying in the wake of the detonation, and he took off running through the chaos. The grenade had ripped apart the doorframe, so he hopped over the burning debris and inside then veered right. He stopped long enough to remove two of the remote bombs from the pack and stuff them in open pocket before continuing on.

Richard: "Two guards in the room on your left. Arguing, it appears."

Seemed it was a theme. Amateurs.

David: "Excellent. They'll be distracted."

Blade in one hand and Daemon in the other, he sneaked into the dimly lit room and closed on the nearest of the two guards. His blade hand wrapped around the man's neck and sliced across it while his gun hand extended over the man's shoulder to shoot the other guard in the face. If the target wore a defensive shield, it buckled under the point-blank force and the man's face...well, David was glad the room was dimly lit for more than one reason.

He dropped a bomb in the corner, checked the hall—though Navick would have alerted him if it was occupied—and continued on.

Richard: "Lots of utility rooms on this hall. Take the next left to reach the heart of the building. First open room is a dining and break room. One person is in there gathering up water packets into a satchel."

David: "They're getting ready to make a run for it."

Richard: *"Looks like."*

When he reached the break room, he leaned inside, shot the man in the base of the neck and kept moving.

Richard: *"Twenty meters ahead take another left, then the second right is the room Tai and three others are holed up in at present."*

David: *"Got it."*

Richard: *"You did hear the part about there being four of them?"*

David: *"I did. But it's a small room, right?"*

Richard: *"Relatively."*

David: *"Perfect—"*

Something slammed into him from behind and sent him sprawling to the floor. A body-sized mass landed on top of him. The glimmer of a gamma blade flashed in his peripheral vision.

He threw all his weight into shoving his shoulder up and back, knocking the attacker off-balance. It bought him a bit of space, which he used to wrench his left arm around and open fire.

Blood splattered on him as he shoved the faint outline of a cloaked body backwards. When it ceased fighting him, he flipped it on its stomach and felt around the waist band for the shield module. He removed it and tossed it down the hall, and a bloodied, now dead terrorist revealed itself.

Richard: *"What happened? "*

David: *"I hate to break it to you, but some of the terrorists have cloaking shields."*

Richard: *"Crap. The thermal seekers won't pick them up unless the bot is practically on top of them."*

David: *"It's fine. I've got this. Ahead and left, second right."*

He leaned against the wall long enough to catch his breath, dropped a bomb on the floor and pressed on, with renewed attention to his surroundings after the unexpected melee.

He didn't actually intend on bursting into the room and opening fire on four people. Not when he had bombs which could do a far more thorough job of dismembering them.

He worked his way down the hall in question to silently approach the door. He stuck a bomb to the right side of it, then to the left. Two additional bombs he'd designated for the rear section of the building, and he should have full coverage.

This time he heard the telltale scuffle of an advancing attacker. Again, he wanted to call them amateurs—stealth was about more than a cloaking shield—but he reminded himself that the amateurs had slaughtered 64,000 innocent civilians and counting.

He spun and painted the hallway in laser fire.

A single retaliatory shot sailed past his head, followed by the thud of a body hitting the floor.

He didn't stop to check this one, because he was running out of time. If they didn't already know, the noise would have alerted the principals that an intruder was running loose in their building. They'd come after him in force or, worse, accelerate their schedule and flee before he could detonate the bombs.

He tossed a bomb through an open door. One to go.

Richard: "Two guards ahead to your right, between you and the rear exit."

He pressed himself against the wall and peeked around the next corner. The hall opened up into a small entryway, where two men stood, guns at the ready.

The distance between him and the targets was such that if they wore defensive shields, the initial fire might not take them out. Dammit, he shouldn't have given up his other grenade to Mendoza.

He readied his blade…and kicked the wall.

A beat later one of the men rounded the corner. David knifed him in the gut and drove him forward, straight into his partner, who was advancing behind him. The three of them crashed into the opposite wall, all flailing limbs and waving weapons.

Richard: "You've got a third guard coming up behind you from the exit."

David managed to wrench his blade up through the man's stomach, and he quit struggling. Behind him, the second man's gaze locked on David.

In one motion David let go of the blade, dropped the body between them, swept his Daemon up and fired into the man's chest as the man's gun arm swung around.

The man's gaze went blank as he slid down the wall.

A thud resounded behind David, and he whirled around to the exit, weapon still raised.

Navick stood in the doorway behind another body crumpled on the floor, a Daemon resting at his side and two holos floating on either side of his face. He shrugged. "I decided I wasn't doing much good acting as your eyes if I couldn't see half the threats. Thought I should come help."

David chuckled raggedly. "You thought right. Thanks." He reached in his pocket, retrieved the last bomb and stuck it on the interior wall by the door. "Let's get out of here and blow this place."

"Music to my ears."

They cleared the area beyond the exit and headed for their former vantage on the hill.

"Uh-oh. Tai and company are on the move. They're coming our way, or the exit's way."

The enemy was about to slip the net. David glanced behind him. They'd covered thirty meters from the building. "Run."

Navick didn't hesitate, and they sprinted toward the outskirts of the compound. Three strides later, he sent the detonation signal.

The shockwave hit his back like a rocket-propelled furnace blast. Then he was airborne. Then the ground was above him. He tucked his body in and landed on his shoulder in a dreadful show of a combat roll.

After blinking woozily a few times, he painfully wrenched his neck up to survey the scene. The entire command center and several of the surrounding buildings were engulfed in flames, their façades breaking apart and collapsing into rubble. "Navick?"

"Over here."

The pained response had come from his left; David pushed up onto his elbows and used his forearms to crawl over to his new friend. One of Navick's pants legs smoldered, and a cut on his fore-head seeped blood, but he looked okay, all things considered.

"You good?"

Navick waved a hand in David's general direction. "I'm good. But it's two beers."

"What?"

"You owe me two beers."

David nodded in weary agreement as the mission comm channel announced the arrival of the reinforcements. "Oh, and by the way? It's nice to meet you."

THE STORY OF AURORA IS COMPLETE, BUT THE STORY OF AMARANTHE IS JUST BEGINNING.

***

"What's past is prologue"
— William Shakespeare

ASTERION NOIR

BOOK 1

EXIN EX MACHINA

Now Available in Print, Ebook & Audiobook
GSJENNSEN.COM/EXIN-EX-MACHINA

***

SUBSCRIBE TO G. S. JENNSEN.'S NEWSLETTER
GSJENNSEN.COM/SUBSCRIBE

Receive new book announcements and stay informed about all the Amaranthe news

Author's Note

I published *Starshine* in March of 2014. In the back of the book I put a short note asking readers to consider leaving a review or talking about the book with their friends. Since that time I've had the unmitigated pleasure of watching my readers do exactly that, and there has never been a more wonderful and humbling experience in my life. There's no way to properly thank you for that support, but know you changed my life and made my dreams a reality.

I'll make the same request now. If you loved *SHORT STORIES OF AURORA RHAPSODY*, tell someone. If you bought the book on Amazon, consider leaving a review. If you downloaded the book off a website with Russian text in the margins and pictures of cartoon video game characters in the sidebar, consider recommending it to others.

As I've said before, reviews are the lifeblood of a book's success, and there is no single thing that will sell a book better than word-of-mouth. My part of this deal is to write a book worth talking about—your part of the deal is to do the talking. If you all keep doing your bit, I get to write a lot more books for you.

This time I'm also going to make a second request. These stories were independently published, written by one person and worked on by a small team of colleagues. Right now there are thousands of writers out there chasing this same dream.

Go to Amazon and surf until you find an author you like the sound of. Take a small chance with a few dollars and a few hours of your time. In doing so, you may be changing those authors' lives by giving visibility to people who until recently were shut out of publishing, but who have something they need to say. It's a revolution, and it's waiting on you.

Lastly, I love hearing from my readers. Seriously. Just like I don't have a publisher or an agent, I don't have "fans." I have **readers** who buy and read my books, and **friends** who do that then reach out to me through email or social media. If you loved the book—or if you didn't—let me know. The beauty of independent publishing is its simplicity: there's the writer and the readers. Without any overhead, I can find out what I'm doing right and wrong directly from you, which is invaluable in making the next book better than this one. And the one after that. And the twenty after that.

Website: www.gsjennsen.com
Wiki: gsj.space/wiki
Email: gs@gsjennsen.com
Twitter: @GSJennsen
Facebook: facebook.com/gsjennsen.author
Goodreads: goodreads.com/gs_jennsen
Instagram: instagram.com/gsjennsen

Find all my books on Amazon:
http://amazon.com/author/gsjennsen

About The Author

G. S. JENNSEN lives somewhere in the U.S., in a locale that may or may not be where she lived the last time she published a book (she's a gypsy at heart), with her husband and two dogs. She has become an internationally bestselling author since her first novel, *Starshine*, was published in March 2014. She has chosen to continue writing under an independent publishing model to ensure the integrity of her series and her ability to execute on the vision she's had for them since their genesis.

While she has been a lawyer, a software engineer and an editor, she's found the life of a full-time author preferable by several orders of magnitude.

When she isn't writing, she's gaming or working out or getting lost in the Colorado mountains that loom large outside the windows in her home. Or she's dealing with a flooded basement, or standing in a line at Walmart reading the tabloid headlines and wondering who all of those people are. Or sitting on her back porch with a glass of wine, looking up at the stars, trying to figure out what could be up there.